"So you bake cookies, huh? I'm impressed."

"I'm glad." Stu moved up behind Zan and put his arms around her waist. His broad hand stroked her stomach lazily, and his breath stirred the hair by her ear. "I'm told I'm very good at it, too." He slid his hand underneath her loose cotton sweater and rested it against her skin.

"I'm sure you are," Zan said faintly.

"The secret is concentration," Stu went on, his voice low. His lips brushed softly against her neck. "And, of course, the right ingredients." His tongue trailed up toward her ear. "Sweetness and spice. And then—"

"And then?" Zan asked breathlessly as she felt his teeth lightly scrape the outside of her ear.

"A very hot oven."

Dear Reader,

Welcome to Silhouette. Experience the magic of the wonderful world where two people fall in love. Meet heroines who will make you cheer for their happiness, and heroes (be they the boy next door or a handsome, mysterious stranger) who will win your heart. Silhouette Romances reflect the magic of love—sweeping you away with books that will make you laugh and cry, heartwarming, poignant stories that will move you time and time again.

In the next few months, we're publishing romances by many of your all-time favorites, such as Diana Palmer, Brittany Young, Emilie Richards and Arlene James. Your response to these authors and other authors of Silhouette Romances has served as a touchstone for us, and we're pleased to bring you more books with Silhouette's distinctive medley of charm, wit and—above all—*romance*.

I hope you enjoy this book and the many stories to come. Experience the magic!

Sincerely,

Tara Hughes
Senior Editor
Silhouette Books

JUDE O'NEILL

Just One Look

Silhouette Romance

Published by Silhouette Books New York
America's Publisher of Contemporary Romance

For Neil

There are no words...

SILHOUETTE BOOKS
300 E. 42nd St., New York, N.Y. 10017

ISBN: 0-373-08464-1

First Silhouette Books printing October 1986

America's Publisher of Contemporary Romance

Printed in the U.S.A.

JUDE O'NEILL

has written everything from radio commercials to book jackets to film reviews, but considers them all a breeze compared to teaching high school English. She tossed aside the glamorous life of an underpaid editor in Manhattan to become a full-time writer. Married to an artist, she divides her time between California and New York.

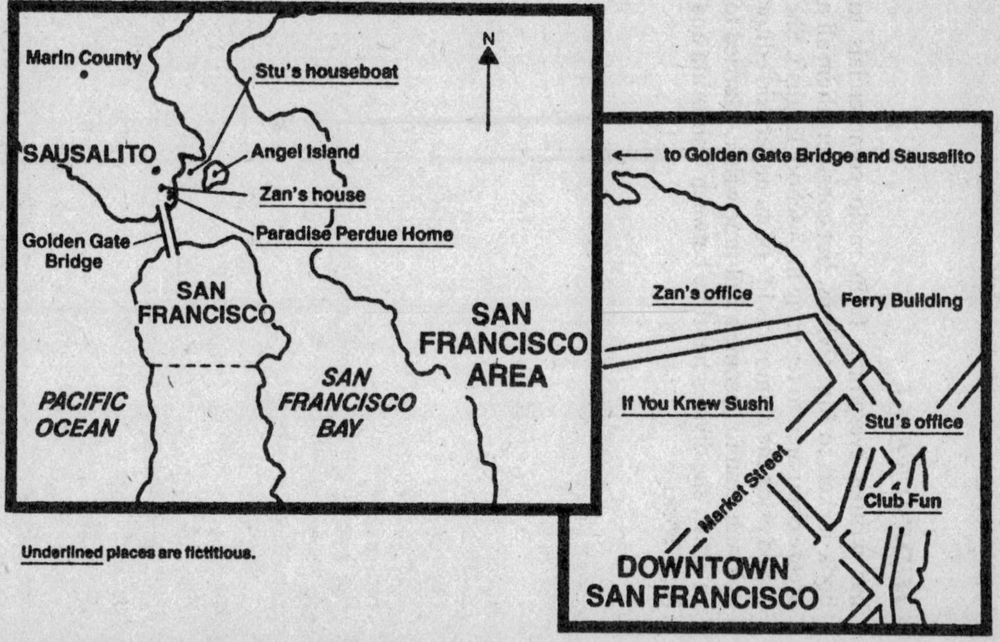

Underlined places are fictitious.

Chapter One

Zan squeezed her way onto the line of cars approaching the Golden Gate Bridge. A solid mass of multicolored metal stretched ahead of her all the way to the tall red-orange towers, and she groaned aloud and checked her watch. At least she still had plenty of time to make it to Sausalito to meet Stewart Temple; she'd bolted out of the office an hour too early from sheer nerves.

Not nerves, Zan, she corrected herself grimly. *Indigestion.* The flutter in her stomach was entirely due to the two chili dogs she'd consumed for lunch to take her mind off this evening. How could she possibly be nervous about a videodate she hadn't wanted to make with a man she was primed to dislike?

She rolled ahead a few inches, considering it an achievement. If this kept up, she might make it to The Oyster Bar by midnight. Though actually, she mused, for once she wouldn't mind being a little late. She caught a glimpse of herself in the rearview mirror and discovered a mischievous gleam in her light brown eyes and a small smile curving her lips at the thought of keeping the arrogant Mr. Temple waiting.

He'd probably be leaning against the bar when she arrived, and he'd be drinking champagne. He'd immediately try to charm her, of course. Taking her hand, he'd hold it for a beat longer than necessary while his deep blue eyes would regard her with seductive intent. His large hand would envelop hers completely and his palm would be rough and cool...

But she wouldn't be disarmed. She'd never been a sucker for tall big-shouldered men with wicked grins; she'd ignore his silken manner and be cool and collected. *I'm Zan Flanders, Mr. Temple,* she'd say briskly. *I'm sorry to get you here under false pretenses, but...* Then she'd calmly explain why she was there.

She'd be able to handle him just fine, if she ever made it across the bridge. Zan sighed and glanced over at the bay for the first time that evening. The sight made her catch her breath. The sun was setting, and the light was a shimmering golden glow that lit up the city buildings in a dazzling white display and lent the cobalt water a coppery sheen. The hills surrounding the bay sloped gently down to cradle it in colors of gold and green.

How long had it been since she'd stopped to enjoy the spectacle of a sunset on San Francisco Bay? Zan gazed out the window as a patch of fog drifted by. And the fog, too—how lovely it was.

She sat up with a start. The evening was perfectly clear, so why was a patch of fog hovering around her car? A honk sounded next to her and she followed the driver's pointing finger to her hood. Clouds of steam were billowing out from under it.

There was no place to pull over on the bridge. Zan pulled the knob to activate her emergency flashers, then rested her head on the steering wheel to avoid meeting the exasperated glances of her fellow commuters. This day had brought her nothing but trouble so far, and it was all Stewart Temple's fault. How had she gotten herself into this? The day had started out familiarly enough with an argument with Mark in his office. She'd been polite and mature about his newest brainstorm, of course....

"Mark, this is the stupidest idea you've ever had."

"I think it's a terrific idea." Mark's desk chair creaked alarmingly as he leaned back and rested his hands on his paunch. "And, well, I do hate to remind you, but I *am* the editor-in-chief of this rag."

"You always pull that one on me. You also believe in absolute monarchy and the divine right of kings." Zan got up restlessly and paced the worn carpet. "This rug looks like one big coffee stain. What color was it originally, anyway? Yellow? Brown? Green? Chartreuse? Do you know they're placing bets on it down in the mail room? I put five dollars on puce."

"You're always a smart aleck when you're trying to change the subject. I went to a lot of trouble to sign you up at Just One Look, you know."

"You mean the videodating service? Who asked you to!"

"And I'm telling you, it'll make a great column. All you have to do is pick a guy who fits your Bachelor of the 80's stereotype—any slimy cad you want—meet him for a drink and give him a chance to answer all those nasty accusations you made about his type in your column. Then you write another witty piece on that, and bingo! We keep the controversy going, not to mention sell lots of magazines. We just have to find someone fairly normal and articulate. I think we're getting close, don't you?"

"Are you kidding? Do you mean Jerry Broder, who left a 'profitable dry cleaning establishment in Hoboken, New Jersey' to come to California to fulfill his potential as a haiku poet? Or Arnold Krebs, from the 'exciting field of insurance,' who'll give me a free consultation if I date him?"

"So they're not exactly what we have in mind..."

"Let's not forget Marty Dweck. His girlfriends call him 'Tiger Man' and he likes 'ladies who know how to let go.' If you think this is going to be such a delightful experience, why don't *you* meet one of them for a drink?"

"I don't think he'd be too pleased if I showed up instead of a chestnut-haired knockout with terrific legs."

Zan leaned on the windowsill and looked down at herself. She was wearing baggy khaki trousers, and it was hard to tell if she had any legs at all. "How can you tell? You're just trying to butter me up."

"I know better than that. I saw them at the magazine softball game this summer. And besides," Mark continued calmly as Zan sighed and looked out the window at downtown San Francisco traffic, "I'm not Zan Flanders, ironic observer of life in the 80's. People aren't panting to hear my opinion on things, as you're making painfully obvious at the moment."

Zan crossed the room to pick up her coffee cup, then threw herself back into her chair. She winced as it shuddered under her slight weight. The dilapidated offices of *Modern Times* were totally at odds with the magazine's lucrative popularity, and it was a running joke with the staff. But she was feeling too irritable to make a joke. "That's just it. I'm an *observer*, Mark. I write about other people's experiences, not my own, and now you want to turn me into queen of the Dating Game!" For emphasis, she pounded on the arm of her chair, which promptly fell off.

Mark peered over his desk at it wordlessly for a moment. Then he shrugged and pushed back the brim of his baseball cap. "Think of it as an interview, not a date. Look Zan, like it or not, you've become a personality in this town, especially since you've done those talk shows. You look into the camera with that Iowa fresh face and those melting-honey eyes of yours and they can't believe how nasty you can be. I'm telling you, they'll love this angle."

"Maybe." Actually, Zan had been surprised at the furor her article had created in the first place. She wound her thick wavy hair into a bun and plucked a pencil off Mark's desk to anchor it there. She'd only written "The Bachelor of the 80's: Or Why I'm Rapidly Turning Into An Old Maid" to exorcise the ghost of Todd once and for all. She'd gotten over the broken engagement years ago, but all she seemed to hear about from friends and readers were men exactly like him. They all wore the same Italian suits, drove the same German cars, and drank the same French wines. But it wasn't just the trappings. Inside, they allowed themselves little room for the messy travails of emotional intimacy. They were too intent on their rapidly rising careers and their dazzling self-sufficient lifestyles. They made attractive and amusing escorts, but what, Zan had wondered in her column, had happened to romance? "To the Bachelor of the 80s," she had concluded, "commitment is a word he uses easily, as in 'I'm not ready for a—', and stretch marks are solid grounds for a breakup. Let's face it, there's always another gourmet cook with an MBA and perfect muscle tone around the corner."

Mark rooted around among the videotapes on his desk and held one up. "Adam Trent. This is the guy, I can feel it. Sounds upscale, articulate, a real man about town." He grinned at Zan's sour look. "Don't panic. I'm not asking you to get involved with the guy. I don't expect the impossible."

"What's that supposed to mean?"

"You said it yourself. You're an observer. You don't treat any man seriously."

"That's not true."

"Ah, this from the columnist who said she'd never date any man over six foot two because he could see the gunk on top of her refrigerator? All I can say is," Mark continued before Zan could defend herself, "that irony can be a useful tool in keeping the heart untouched." He gave Zan a significant look over the top of his glasses and loaded the tape.

A mild-looking, impeccably dressed man appeared on the screen. He cleared his throat, adjusted his Windsor-knotted tie, and began. "I'm looking for a classically beautiful woman who enjoys fine wines, nouvelle cuisine, tax law, and entering mud wrestling competitions."

Mark avoided Zan's grin and stabbed at the eject button. "The next one should be an improvement. His name is..." he squinted at the label before loading the tape, "Sludge?"

An intense man in an orange T-shirt nodded jerkily at the camera. His spiked hair was a startlingly bright shade of green. "If you're into slam dancing—"

Zan laughed and stood up as Mark ejected the tape. "I hate to tear myself away, but I have to go turn off my phone and edit my column. It's been fun, though."

"Don't go yet. One more." Mark scrambled back to his desk and pawed through the remaining tapes. "Aha! Stewart Temple. Not a bad name. Beats 'Sludge,' anyway." Motioning to Zan to sit again, Mark loaded the tape. "I hope this one's halfway normal," he muttered to himself before pressing play. "At this point, I hope he's from Earth."

"My name is Stewart Temple and I'm thirty-five years old today," a deep voice growled. Zan sat up slowly, spilling a little coffee on her sweater. A rather large disheveled man in a faded blue T-shirt and a tweed jacket that had seen better days was sprawled in a desk chair, holding a glass of champagne. He looked harried and irritable, and not very happy about being there. He ran a hand through his thick jet-black hair, which was brushed straight off his forehead. Zan could see that it was a little long in back, brushing against his collar. He had a substantial nose with a small bump in it, a surprisingly full mouth, and what looked like a two-day's growth of beard. And Zan could tell, even on videotape, that he had a pair of stunning blue eyes. Right now they were glaring disagreeably right at her.

"I like to play basketball and I like to sail. I like to work and I do it constantly, at least when I don't have to deal with too many interruptions." Suddenly a twinkle appeared in those blue eyes, and Zan sat up even straighter. Her heart was beating at double-time, and she leaned forward. A smile seemed to be dancing around one corner of Stewart Temple's mobile mouth, and she found herself beginning to smile back foolishly, just at the promise of it. One end of his mouth curled up, and he looked off-camera, as if directing his remarks to someone there. "What I don't want, or need, is help meeting women. I seem to have more women than I can handle. And by the way, I *like* being single, no matter what they might want to believe. I like my life just the way it is." He took a sip of champagne and raised his glass to the camera, his blue eyes seeming to lock onto hers with a mocking challenge. "But happy hunting to you, folks."

The image clicked off and the sharp fuzz of empty tape replaced it. Zan found that she had risen without realizing it, and was standing stock still in front of the screen. What an arrogant, obnoxious, confusing man! If he didn't need any help meeting women, why had he joined a dating service? He was practically *taunting* women to call him for a date. And he would probably get plenty of responses, Zan admitted ruefully. He had a kind of devastating good looks that were not unappealing coupled with his slightly rumpled charm. But he seemed to be well aware of his effect. "I seem to have more than I can handle," indeed!

"Zan? What do you think?"

Mark's question barely penetrated her absorption in Stewart Temple. Zan went to the videotape machine and rewound a portion of the tape. "But happy hunting to you, folks," Stewart Temple said again, his eyes gleaming wickedly.

She pressed the freeze frame button and captured him raising his champagne glass at her. Zan picked up her cold coffee and toasted his flickering image. "The Bachelor of the 80's," she said softly. "Here's looking at you, kid."

But now Stewart Temple was nowhere to be found. Twenty-nine years of living had certainly taught Zan that life had its share of absurd moments, but this was positively surreal. "I'm standing next to an eight-foot cactus, trying to hail a roller-skating waiter in a Sausalito singles bar while being stood up by my video date," she murmured to herself. Somehow the situation didn't seem any less bizarre when she said it out loud. How dare he not show up, when she'd spent the past forty-five minutes in a frenzy of impatience, being towed off the bridge to a service station and then dashing through the Sausalito hills to make it on time? She'd skidded into The Oyster Bar, tousled and wheezing, only seven minutes late, already preparing her apologies.

And he wasn't there. Maybe he'd left after a few minutes. Maybe his secretary hadn't given him her message. Or maybe Zan was just one of hordes of women standing in bars all over the Bay Area waiting for Stewart Temple to show up, flash his wicked grin, twinkle his blue eyes, and disarm them completely. Somehow that wouldn't surprise her a bit.

She ordered a beer from the pirouetting waiter and decided that she'd actually be relieved if he didn't show up. She was only here under duress, after all. She took a sip of beer resolutely, glad she had her feelings under control. Then she heard his voice.

Her heart actually seemed to stop beating for a moment at the sound. Then it began to thump at a rather quick gallop, and Zan sank onto a vacant stool as the deep voice argued irritably with the maître d' behind her.

"Calm *down*, Zan," she whispered to herself fiercely, but her heart continued to beat in the same erratic rhythm. The elegant woman next to her gave her a strange look, probably convinced she was unstable.

She *was* unstable, Zan realized, she was practically reeling. She told herself her nervousness was ridiculous;

she'd only heard his voice. But the air seemed to be thicker, more electric with his presence, and a provocative thrill was skittering up her spine. Zan took a deep breath to collect herself, then slowly slid off her stool and headed for Stewart Temple.

His back was to her, but she recognized the wide set of his shoulders in the same rumpled jacket he'd worn on his tape. He towered over the small sleek maître d' like a friendly but potentially menacing bear. Zan studied the tense line of his shoulders and decided that if ever a man could indicate bad temper by the back of him, Stewart Temple could. She could see him gesturing with his large hands as the maître d' shrugged, unmoved. Frustrated, he ran his fingers through his combed-back hair, and suddenly it was as though she'd seen the gesture a thousand times instead of only once before; it had the familiar tug of the habit of a long-lost friend. She paused a few feet behind him and finally was able to catch his words.

"Yes, yes, I know it's a reserved parking space, but it's impossible to park anywhere else. I'll only be a few minutes, I just have to find someone, and . . ." He continued in a lowered tone, and Zan saw him slip a folded bill into the maître d's hand. The dapper man retreated, and he began to scan the room.

Zan approached him warily; she wondered if he would bite. She put her hand on his shoulder, then withdrew it quickly. "Stewart Temple?"

He spun around, and suddenly Zan found herself looking into the clearest blue eyes she'd ever seen, so blue that she felt refreshed, as if she'd dived into a cerulean pool on a hot summer day. His complexion looked surprisingly fair against their intensity, and the slight black stubble on his cheeks emphasized the paleness as well. Black Irish, Zan decided, and wondered if his temper matched his looks. The vivid contrast of his skin and hair along with his large frame made him seem overwhelming and volatile, as if he might go off in a rage at any moment.

The intense eyes swept her body and lingered on her rather battered sneakers with that slight lift to one corner of his mouth. Then, as quickly as it had appeared, the amused look was gone and replaced with the more familiar scowl.

Zan decided to ignore it and forge ahead. "I'm Zan Flanders," she said pleasantly, holding out her hand.

He shook it briskly and then dropped it as though it burned his skin. "Call me Stu." He glanced at his watch impatiently. "Look, I don't have time for this."

Zan had to grit her teeth to hold on to her smile. "Nice to meet you, too."

Stu gestured out the window to an ancient station wagon with wood paneling on the sides, parked haphazardly by the curb. "I've been informed that I'm not allowed to park there and I only gave the maître d' a buck, so I figure that gives me about five minutes, tops." He swiped at a fern that dangled in front of his face. "I hate this place," he muttered to himself, then returned his attention to Zan. "I tried to get you all afternoon to cancel this thing. Don't you ever check your messages?"

"Only when I have to."

Stu nodded his head rapidly, looking at her intently. "Zan Flanders. What kind of a name is that? What's your real first name?"

"Alexandra."

Stu nodded again. "Alexandra. I like it better."

"Too bad," Zan shot back, feeling ridiculous.

"The thing is, my secretary made this date for me. She's new, and well, nothing personal, but I really don't want to be here."

"That makes two of us," Zan responded sweetly. "Look, it's only been a minute and a half, maybe the maître d' will give you seventy-five cents back."

Stu looked startled for a second. Then he grinned at her, a slow appreciative grin with a mocking edge to it that sent a delectable sharp thrill all through her, making her feel just a bit off balance. One eyebrow lifted as he gave her another assessing glance. "Maybe we should sit down after all," he said.

Chapter Two

Stu turned without another word and led the way to a table by the window. Zan guessed that she was supposed to follow obediently, like a faithful dog. The man was giving new meaning to the term arrogance. She walked over and banged her beer down on the table with the controlled force of her irritation.

Unperturbed, Stu glanced at the label. "Good choice. I approve."

"Now I'll be able to sleep tonight," Zan said.

Stu's eyes crinkled at the corners as he smiled, and she was unexpectedly charmed by the sight of a chipped front tooth. The setting sun slanted through the window and lit his face, making his skin look almost translucent and his eyes a paler, though no less startling, blue. Zan felt a curious liquidity in her stomach. She was relieved when Stu looked away to try and hail a passing waiter, who zoomed by without braking.

"I hate this place," Stu announced again. "I always expect a waiter to do a flying camel into my drink. Underdone fish, overpriced champagne, overdone decor..."

"You'd better talk lower; you could get yourself strangled by a fern."

Stu smiled again, and to defuse the charm of that smile—she certainly didn't want to start liking him—Zan continued, "Actually, I thought it would be exactly the type of place you would like. It's Sausalito's most popular singles place, you know. Happy hunting grounds and all that." Stu looked puzzled, then annoyed, and Zan leaned back in her chair, satisfied, as he ordered a beer from the waiter.

She reached for a carrot on the tray of crudités in front of them, but she found it difficult to chew and swallow; the carrot tasted dry and dusty in her throat. It was just that Stu was so infuriating, so...large, sitting there at the tiny cocktail table. His knee was perilously close to hers underneath it, and she drew her legs closer to her body. She felt a strange need to protect herself from him.

"So you're Zan Flanders, the woman with the silly name who never checks her messages. You're not what I expected at all."

Stu looked her over lazily, and Zan willed away the flicker of heat that licked at her insides underneath his slow gaze. "Didn't you see my tape?"

"Didn't have the curiosity or the time." Stu shook his head as if to clear it. "Look, I should explain how I got here. I never signed up at a videodating service. For my thirty-fifth birthday some friends of mine came to my office with several bottles of champagne. Somehow during the course of the evening they decided it would be fun if we all made mock tapes about ourselves for an imaginary dating service. Jack, my assistant, used to make money taping for some service a few years ago. Anyway, he shot the four of us. I was literally pushed in front of that camera."

"Ah, that explains your tape. Most of the men I saw tried to show their best side, but you were pretty cranky and flip."

"That *is* my best side." Stu grinned. "It was all very silly. My friends have some idea that I need Ms. Right to humanize me or something, so they got together with my assistant and sent the tape to Just One Look. It was one of my birthday presents."

"There's no Ms. Right among all those women you can't handle?"

"Did I say that?" Stu looked bemused. "I was feeling a little out of focus from the champagne. I was referring to my three friends. They each have about thirty years on me, but they each have about three times my energy. I could have murdered them when they told me what they'd done. I'm sorry to have wasted your time—"

"Well, actually—"

"I'm not interested in dating. I'm very busy with my work, and I certainly would never apply to a videodating service. I don't need to pay a fee to...what I mean is, the people who have to join these types of things tend to be—"

"Unattractive and desperate?"

"Well, I seem to have met the exception." Stu smiled uneasily.

"Mmmm, charming of you to say so."

"Actually, you're a very attractive woman. Now that you're here, maybe you should give this place a try."

"I don't think I need your help to find a date, Mr. Temple," Zan said evenly. "Or are you looking for a fee to set me up with one?"

"You shouldn't be embarrassed. I'm sure that many men would find you attractive. Let me give you a piece of advice, though. On the next date, you could wear something a little more flattering."

"I'll wear my negligee."

"Maybe some heels instead of those sneakers. Of course it's impossible to tell if there's a pair of legs underneath those pants, but—"

"Mr. Temple," Zan interrupted icily, "there's nothing I'd enjoy more than a fashion consultation with a man who's a stranger to his razor and has apparently never heard of the concept of dry cleaning, but I should tell you that I didn't apply to the service either. I'm doing an article on the self-absorbed single man of today, and you seemed to fit the bill. This was to be an interview, but obviously we can't—"

"Ms. Flanders," Stu broke in with exaggerated politeness, "I did not mean to insult you. I don't even know you. I'm a busy man whose employee made a date for me I had no time to keep. I have too many important things waiting for me to—"

"What exactly is it that you do, Mr. Temple? It seems to be rather crucial. Brain surgery? Nuclear waste disposal? Public relations?"

"I'm a film and video producer."

Zan nodded sagely. "Oh. I was close. I realize now that the survival of the free world is hanging by a thread while you sit here and make such charming conversation."

Stu's eyes took on the hue of a twilight frost. His fingers curled around his beer, and Zan was annoyed to find that she noticed how square and strong they were. He took a deep breath. "I make documentaries, Ms. Flanders, and I don't think I have to justify the importance of my work to you. Or the use of my time." He leaned forward slightly, and the knee that had been hovering so close to hers made contact. Zan felt a shudder of excitement so intense she felt dizzy. *It was just a knee, Zan,* she told herself, slightly hysterical. She quickly tucked her legs in again.

"What is it that you write about, Ms. Flanders?" Stu's voice was lazy and slow, but she sensed the dangerous undercurrent.

"I write a humor column for *Modern Times* magazine. I deal with modern trends, relationships, society..."

"I see. A lighthearted look at videodating, and the like. Not exactly brain surgery, is it?"

Zan sucked in her breath. "I don't have to justify the importance of my work to you either, Mr. Temple. Just because I'm a humorist doesn't mean I can't tackle serious subjects. I don't know about your films—"

"My last film was 'Born of the Troubles,' about the children of Northern Ireland." Stu paused, then asked idly, "What was your last column on?"

"It was a piece on health clubs called 'Narcissism is An Aerobic Activity.' But—"

"Before that I did 'Waves of Grain,' about farmers in Nebraska who were losing their land. How about you?"

"'If There's a VCR Revolution How Come Everyone's In My Movie Line?'"

Stu leaned back in his chair. "Your column sounds very...entertaining."

Zan leaned back as well. The strange excitement that had so unnerved her had changed into fury, and she welcomed it. It was a feeling she could handle. "How many people have seen your films, Stu?" she asked lightly. If he had been familiar with her interview technique, Stu would have known that the use of his first name meant she was quietly moving in for the kill.

"I don't know, exactly."

"Let me see. Your films play at small art houses and run for about two weeks, right? An audience of critics and socially-conscious intellectuals?"

"They've won several awards."

"I'm sure," Zan said soothingly, and was glad to see Stu bristle. "Do you know how many people read my column every week?"

Stu waved his hand impatiently. "Plenty, I'm sure. *Modern Times* has a huge circulation, I know that. But what does your column do for your readers?"

"Maybe it makes them laugh."

"But does it make them think?"

"Maybe it does that too," Zan replied furiously. "How would you know?" She reached over for an olive. It was a trick she'd learned from conducting hostile interviews; she tried to put something in her mouth when she began to lose her temper, since invariably she'd say something she'd regret. She chewed vigorously while Stu watched her, amused. His eyes lingered on her mouth before returning to meet her furious gaze.

"Look," he said, "I think you might be overreacting a bit. Of course there's a place for your kind of light reporting—"

"While you do the important stuff?" Zan asked angrily around her olive. Darn, it was the kind with a pit. How could she be cutting and sarcastic with an olive pit in her mouth? "I think your implication—"

"I didn't imply anything negative. I never said—"

"You didn't have to! I got the message!" She pushed the olive pit to one side of her cheek with her tongue. If Stu would only look away, she'd be able to cough politely and spit it into her napkin unobtrusively. But he didn't oblige; his cool eyes continued to rest on her face.

Flustered and annoyed, Zan continued the argument while she looked around discreetly for a place to deposit the pit. "And furthermore, throughout the ages, humor—" Noticing her dilemma, Stu leaned over and cupped his palm under her chin, and Zan gratefully spit the pit into his hand so she could continue with her point. "—has dealt with many of society's injustices—" She stopped abruptly, aghast, when she realized what she'd done. A small gasp escaped her and Stu chuckled.

"I... I'm sorry. I didn't mean to..." she stammered.

"Just lending a helping hand. Don't apologize, I enjoyed it."

Stu's amused eyes looked into her embarrassed ones, and together they glanced down at the damp wrinkled pit nestled in his large palm. It was mute evidence of the familiar intimacy of her action and Zan felt her cheeks flush. She'd just spit out her food residue into the hand of a man she'd only known for five minutes.

They both looked up again simultaneously and the mood changed. Suddenly their gazes met and tangled in a mutual acknowledgement of the heat between them. The light and noise of the bar dropped away and Zan was now aware only of Stu, of his clear eyes telling her that he wanted her, so plainly that she was both shocked and excited. She felt giddy and lightheaded, and she was completely, utterly mad with what she now knew was desire. This was something so new, so overwhelming, that it lit up every nerve ending, every inch of skin.

She tore her gaze away, embarrassed. The man had just accepted her olive pit, not proposed running away to Acapulco. Zan stood up quickly and locked her knees so they wouldn't tremble. "It's obvious that neither one of us wants to be here," she said, summoning up every ounce of strength to put force in her voice. Stu was looking at her, head cocked, faintly smiling at her obvious discomfiture. A new jolt of anger shot through her. The man refused to take her seriously for a moment.

"I'm sorry I wasted so much of your valuable time," she continued. "I'm sure that there must be something depressing going on somewhere that you have to document. I have to get home so I can practice being frivolous." Zan turned toward the door, but had only gone a few steps when she spun around and went back to the table. "By the way," she said sweetly, "they're towing your car."

"He's an arrogant, insensitive, patronizing, pompous, rude . . . uh. . . . arrogant . . ."

"You said that."

"Slime mold!" Spent, Zan flung herself into the chair at the foot of Mark's desk. The recently reattached arm fell with a clunk.

Mark looked at her balefully over his glasses. "You are hell on the furniture, you know that? How are you able to come up with all those adjectives?"

"I'm a writer. Besides, I looked them up in the thesaurus this morning." Zan took a sip of her coffee. "Did I mention pretentious?"

"I don't think so."

"At least I confined myself to being snide and making a fool of myself."

"Sounds like a fun date. Now would you please listen to me? I'm trying to tell you something impor—"

"The nerve! Giving me advice on how to attract men."

"You know that the television version of the magazine has been in the works for some time. Well, it finally got the go-ahead. It's going to be called 'Modern Times on Screen.' Local to start, but there's plans for syndication. Great, huh?"

"Terrific. Who does he think he is, anyway?"

"Now here's the good part."

"Telling me to wear heels."

"You know how I keep telling you how great you come across on TV?"

"Uh huh. I should have belted him." Zan rose and started to pace.

"I screened all those appearances you've done for the producer. She loved them."

"I couldn't help being a little nasty in return."

"So then I pitched her the idea for the interview you're going to do with a sample Bachelor of the 80's. She thought it was 'fabulous,' so we talked about expanding it for the show. We'll pick a bunch of guys from the tapes, and then each one will take you out on his favorite 'date' while you interview him about why he's chosen videodating as a way to meet women, how he feels about being single, and so on. It'll be a mini-documentary, five to ten minutes each week. And you'll be the on-air talent."

Zan stopped pacing. "Me?"

"You. You'll be great. I guaranteed the producer."

"I don't know." Zan sighed worriedly, then decided to think about it later. She resumed her pacing. "You know," she said confidingly, "he isn't even as good-looking as he thinks he is. Not really."

"The best part is that I weaseled my way in as executive producer of your segment. The only hitch is that I have to find someone to *really* produce it. The show is so new that they don't have much of a crew, so they want me to freelance it."

"He's busy trying to save humanity when he can't even carry on a friendly conversation."

"So all I need is a—"

"Imagine being such a snob about being a—"

"Hot shot documentary producer." Zan and Mark spoke the words together. She spun around and they stared at each other silently for a moment. Mark began to rise, slowly.

"No," Zan said.

"Is he any good?"

"*He* thinks so."

"I need someone good. I have to look good on this."

"Mark, he'll never do it. It's too frivolous. Haven't you been listening to me?"

"We'll have to check him out, make sure he's good. Then you can call him—"

"Mark!"

"Of course I've been listening to you, sweetie. The slime mold sounds promising."

"No," Zan said with finality. "No way. I don't ever want to talk to Stu Temple again."

"Temple Productions."

"Stewart Temple, please."

"Speaking."

"This is Zan Flanders. I'm calling—"

"To apologize. Good. I might consider accepting it, if—"

"Consider it if you wish, Mr. Temple, but an apology is not forthcoming from me. You, on the other hand, can feel free to do so."

"You called me up to tell me I could apologize to you?"

"I called you up because I have a job offer for you."

"A what?"

"My magazine is starting a television show. I'm doing a mini-documentary series on it and we need someone to produce it."

"You've got to be kidding. Do you know what kind of work I do?"

"Yes," Zan answered dryly, "I got a complete run down on it last night, remember? But I also remember discussing that your films aren't exactly boffo at the box office, and I understand that you do work on contract occasionally. I imagine that the magazine will pay well."

There was a pause on the other end of the phone and Zan switched her receiver from one hand to the other to wipe her perspiring palm on her pants. She wished that Stu would go ahead and turn her down. He wasn't going to accept, was he? The thought made her foot tap even faster. She pictured him on the other end of the phone, considering her offer. There was, she felt sure, a frown on his handsome face, and he probably still hadn't shaved. Perhaps he was running his hand through the sleek brushed-back hair.

"What's the subject, anyway? And would I have any say as to the content?"

Zan hesitated. "My editor and I will decide the content. Your suggestions will be welcomed, of course. The piece is a look at the single man today, what he thinks about marriage, women, commitment. We'll be conducting interviews at various popular singles spots around the city. The format will be like a date."

"And you're Bachelorette Number One?"

"I wouldn't put it that way, exactly."

"I'll be shooting in sushi bars and dance clubs? Lots of talk about 'realistic expectations' and 'being open to experience'?" Stu's voice brimmed with humor, and a small chuckle turned into a full, hearty laugh. Zan would have been tempted to call it infectious if she wasn't so far removed from laughter herself. It went on for several long moments, long enough for her to get quite angry.

"I take it the answer is no."

Another guffaw sputtered through the wire. "I'm sorry," Stu said in a choked voice, "I just—"

"Don't apologize," Zan said furiously. "A simple 'no thanks' would have been sufficient. Goodbye, Mr. Temple." Without waiting for his chuckles to subside, she slammed down the receiver.

The only cure for such an upsetting afternoon was Double Chocolate Fudge with Chocolate-Covered Pralines from Mamie's Ice Cream Parlor, Zan knew, so she'd already stopped off to pick up a pint on her way up the hill that evening. She'd spent the ride home on the ferry gloomily watching the water churn around the boat, and thinking it was a good approximation of the state of her insides.

A hot bath had helped a little. Zan pulled the plug in the tub and watched the water spiral down the drain. She stepped out and rubbed herself vigorously with her thickest towel. Already laid out on her bed were her most comfortable at-home clothes, a fleecy pink sweatshirt that hung almost to her knees, pink leggings, and thick yellow socks. She was determined to pamper herself and enjoy her night at home, without any thoughts of the irritating Stu Temple to interfere. She dressed quickly, gathered her damp hair into a ponytail, and padded downstairs toward the kitchen, stopping in the living room on the second level to turn up the volume on the Bach concertos she'd put on for their soothing qualities.

Her house always made her feel comforted, too. Her brother had asked her to house-sit for him when he'd left for Alaska seven years before, and she was still here; it had become her home. It was a typical older Sausalito small wooden house. Built on three levels, it clung tenaciously to the steep hillside. Each level held only two rooms and a small terrace, but the three flights gave Zan a feeling of space. Her bedroom on the top floor felt like an aerie, far removed from such mundane matters as her office on the second level and the kitchen on the bottom. Outside the windows and French doors on every floor was the ever-changing panorama of San Francisco Bay, with its soft golden hills and aquamarine water and the glow of the white city across the water. Tonight the city lights were obscured by a thick fog that rubbed against the windowpanes; only the soft amber glow of the hillside houses closest to hers were visible through the dense white mist.

Zan shivered as she looked out, though the house was as warm as toast; she was glad to be inside on such a night. Leaving the living room, she continued downstairs to the kitchen. She spooned ice cream into her favorite blue bowl and, sighing happily, went into the adjoining dining room and sank into a chair. She swung her legs up on the table and balanced the bowl on her lap while she reached for the pleasantly fat novel she was trying to get through.

She was just lifting the first heaping spoonful to her lips when she heard the sound of footsteps on the terrace outside. Zan's heartbeat accelerated rapidly and thumped against her ribs. She tried to remember if the door to the terrace was locked; she often neglected to do it since the climb down through the underbrush of the hill to get access to the lowest level would prove daunting to the most agile burglar. Slowly, silently, she tiptoed over to the door to peek through the curtain on its window. Just as she reached it, three heavy knocks resounded through the room and she jumped in alarm.

"Who is it?" she hissed.

"Stu Temple. Open up, it's freezing out here."

Zan opened the door warily and Stu strode inside, bringing a blast of cold and mist with him. "You have the Brandenberg Concertos going so loud you wouldn't be able to hear a mob breaking down your front door. I had to hack my way through a jungle to get down here." Stu brushed some leaves off his gray sweatshirt and contemplated a dirt stain on the knee of his faded jeans. Zan noticed that they were snug along his hips and thighs, and for the first time realized that Stu, for all his size, had a lean athleticism that was decidedly appealing.

"I thought you were a burglar."

"What were you going to do, spoon me to death?"

Zan realized she was brandishing her ice cream spoon like a weapon. She put her hand behind her back. "What are you doing here? Go away."

"I'm sorry if I frightened you. I wanted to talk with you, and I kept getting your blasted machine, so I took a chance and came over. Are you busy?"

"Yes, I am, as a matter of fact, so if you don't mind..." Zan's voice trailed off as she saw Stu's glance move behind her and take in her heaping bowl of ice cream. Her face flushed. Damn the man! As far as she was concerned, it was a female prerogative to consume an entire pint of ice cream instead of dinner in absolute secrecy.

Stu stepped around her to examine the bowl, and he turned back to her happily. His customary cranky look had softened; he looked almost boyish, and infinitely attractive. "Double Chocolate Fudge with Chocolate-Covered Pralines, right? You go to Mamie's, too." He held out his hand for her spoon. "It's my favorite."

Zan kept her spoon behind her back. "Then you can go back down the hill and get your own. I don't want you here. I want you—"

"Oh, I want you, too," Stu said wickedly, "but first I want some ice cream."

Zan stopped, her lips slightly parted. For the life of her, she couldn't think of a thing to say.

"Of course," Stu went on innocently, "I'm also fond of Black Forest with real cherries."

"I want you to tell me why you're here, and then leave, because..."

"Or Chocolate Graham Cracker with real bits of cookie in it."

"That's a new flavor." Zan approached the table slowly.

"It's terrific. I'll treat you to a cone sometime if you let me share your bowl. Were you going to eat this whole thing by yourself? It looks like a whole pint." Stu shook his head in mock alarm, and his eyes examined her figure. "It's a wonder you manage to look so..."

"Oh, all right," Zan said quickly. She handed him her spoon and went to get one for herself, then returned to pull up a chair and dip her spoon alongside Stu's. They ate the first bite in reverent silence, then Stu spoke.

"First of all, I'm sorry about losing control on the phone today. You may not know it, but I usually have more finesse than that with potential clients."

"Now it's my turn to laugh."

"Don't be nasty, now, I'm trying to apologize. The topic just seemed to be a little, uh, frothy for me. But after careful consideration, and a meeting with my accountant, I've decided to accept your offer, but only on two conditions."

Zan captured a praline and crunched on it thoughtfully. "And they are?"

"First, the top rate for video producers in the city. You get what you pay for."

"I'm not authorized to negotiate that," Zan said slowly, "but I don't think it will be a problem." She scooped up another praline.

"Good. Second, I want you to stop hogging all the pralines." Zan looked up, annoyed, but Stu was grinning at her so warmly her heart lurched and a sharp retort died on her lips.

She cleared her throat. "What else do you want?"

"A glass of milk. Have any?"

"Yes. No. I don't know. Go ahead and look." Stu got up and headed for the kitchen, and Zan cringed, suddenly remembering what he'd find in the refrigerator. A bottle of prepared Bloody Mary mix from a Christmas brunch she had last year and an outdated container of yogurt.

Stu peered inside. "Aha—the domestic type, I see." He removed the carton of yogurt, grimaced, and flipped it into the garbage can. Then his head disappeared into the refrigerator again. "You could do carbon dating on this stuff. Is it always this empty?"

"Sometimes I add leftover cartons of Chinese take-out for variety."

"Got any coffee?"

"Beans in the cannister on the counter. And the grinder's next to it."

"Cinnamon?"

"I'm not sure. Spices are above the stove."

Zan got up and put on the kettle while Stu ground the coffee beans and added a pinch of cinnamon. She leaned against the counter while he dumped the mixture into the coffee filter.

"Are you going to tell me what your other condition is?"

"Sure." Stu hunted around in the cupboard until he found two cups he liked. Zan noticed he selected her favorite English bone china patterned with forget-me-nots. It was a choice that pleased her; perhaps there was a delicate side to Stu's bulldozer personality after all.

Stu turned around and caught her watching him, and he returned her stare, his eyes suddenly smoky and intent. His gaze traveled slowly over her body, making her feel a little ridiculous in her ponytail and sweatshirt. She felt curiously vulnerable in her stocking feet. "You do manage to distract me, Zan Flanders," Stu murmured, shaking his head. He moved closer.

Zan took a step backward. She'd felt very cozy a moment before, watching Stu bustle companionably around her kitchen. She'd admired his forearms, revealed by his pushed-up sleeves, and her eye had approvingly noted the lean lines of hip and muscular thigh underneath his jeans. She'd even inched over on the counter to surreptitiously get a better look at his rear view. But now the attributes she'd admired from a safe distance were stalking her, and the gleam of determination in Stu's eyes boded no easy escape. "Aren't you going to make the coffee?" she asked helpfully.

"In a minute." Stu came nearer until they were standing toe to toe. Zan looked up at him and bumped into his crooked nose. He reached behind her and ran his hand down the length of her ponytail, then hung on lightly, his fingers twined through her thick hair. His soft mouth was only inches from hers, and Zan felt a delicious panic flutter through her. She ducked her head to avoid his gaze.

Stu tugged very gently on her ponytail to bring her chin up. He looked down at her through half-closed eyelids. "I have some business to discuss with you," he said huskily, "but I think it's hard for both of us to concentrate." His hand dropped to her neck and he lazily stroked the wispy tendrils there. "Why don't you let me kiss you and get it over with? Then we can go ahead and get down to business."

His words seemed to knock the wind out of her, and Zan told her legs to move, but they didn't obey. Instead of carrying her out of reach of his arms, they stayed right where they were. And instead of refusing Stu's request, her voice made quite a different reply. "All right," she said.

Chapter Three

Stu's fingers slid slowly around to cup her face. His eyes were bright and watchful, making Zan feel somehow like a deer caught in a car's headlights; she hung suspended before him, quivering and vulnerable. Her breath came short as he gazed at her parted lips. Then, with slow and exquisite care, he bent his head and brought his mouth to hers.

He kissed her softly, experimentally, as if he had all the time in the world to enjoy her. He tasted of chocolate and smelled of spice, and Zan found herself melting into his embrace, her heart beating wildly, as the gentle, exploratory kiss went on. Desire shimmered through her, as fine and delicate as crystal, and she shivered as Stu's hands ran down her back to the base of her spine, where he linked his fingers together to hold her against him.

The light pressure of his hands forced her whole body up against his, and the subtle contact of chest against chest, thigh against thigh, made their breath come quicker and they deepened the kiss. The yielding quality of Stu's full mouth changed to something harder and more insistent. His tongue roamed the soft textures of her mouth and his hands brought her even closer up against him.

Zan moaned into his mouth, she couldn't help it, and her arms stole around him to run her hands with intoxicating freedom over the muscles of his back. She sucked gently on the velvety smoothness of his lower lip, causing Stu to inhale sharply. He tugged her sweatshirt up until his hands could slide underneath it and touch the soft skin of her back. The feel of his fingers on her bare skin was an electric jolt. She started, but the rough warmth of his hands brought her back into the tantalizing rhythm of the kiss. She lost herself in it, but somehow was able to track each separate sensation: the abrasiveness of his cheek, his fingers tracing the ridge of her spine, the unfamiliar, drugging smell of him.

Just when it seemed they would have to give themselves up totally to the embrace, when they would have to cling to each other in complete surrender to its power, Stu broke the contact. His lips remained poised above hers for a small space of a moment before drawing away. His hands slid out from underneath her sweatshirt and swung back to his sides.

"I was wrong," he said huskily. "A kiss isn't going to end this. But if we're going to work together, we should stop before we go any further. Maybe we'd better—"

"Forget it." Zan was surprised at how strong her voice sounded. Stu's withdrawal had left her dazed and shaken. She felt warm and pliant, and her legs seemed unable to support her fluid, boneless body. She leaned against the counter and willed herself under control. She mustn't let Stu overwhelm her this way. Obviously he was able to control his reaction to her; he could calmly break off that dizzying, devastating kiss and not pursue it. He hadn't been swept away. His cool mind had been ticking off the reasons they shouldn't be kissing while she'd been moaning like a mournful cow.

She took a deep breath and added offhandedly, "Besides, it's ridiculous to think that we could get along for very long. Considering our differences, it's better to keep our distance."

Stu narrowed his eyes at her. He shrugged and put his hands in his back pockets. "You're right, of course. The strain of the two of us working together is going to drive us crazy, anyway. The kiss was a mistake. Let's forget it."

"It's forgotten." But as Zan turned away from him, she knew she had lied. She would never, ever forget it. Her body still thrummed with it. "Why don't we get back to business?" she asked lightly.

The shrill whistle of the kettle made them start. Stu went over and turned off the burner, then poured the water over the coffee grounds. When he spoke, his voice was cool and even.

"Remember I told you about how three older women friends of mine had enrolled me in Just One Look?" At her nod, he continued, "Amelia, Bertie and Faye all live in the Paradise Perdue Home for Retired Actresses. Ever hear of it?"

Zan shook her head. "I think I'd remember that name."

Stu poured coffee into the cups. His square fingers handled the china delicately as he handed a cup to her. "Paradise Perdue was a fairly successful actress in the thirties. She usually played a dizzy society type dripping with diamonds. Probably because she *was* a dizzy society type dripping with diamonds. Anyway, as she got older, parts got fewer, and she finally retired up here in Sausalito, to a big old Victorian house by the bay. Her friends started coming up from Hollywood for weekends. They were older actresses too, and they all had problems getting parts as they got older. This infuriated Paradise, and that's how her Home for Retired Actresses was born."

"Is she still alive?"

"She died seven years ago. She'd set up a foundation before she died, but she unfortunately put the administration of funds into the hands of her son, Dwayne. Inflation has eaten away at the yearly stipend for some time, but he's refused to increase it. The women can't afford to fix the house, and it's fallen into disrepair. Now he's run through his inheritance and is trying to cut back the amount. The women have been hanging on by a thread, and this could break it. He's backed by some powerful legal counsel, and they could lose everything."

"How awful. What can be done?"

"I think if there's enough publicity about the issue, Dwayne will back off. That's why I'm doing a film on them. But as you said last night, my films don't exactly reach millions. And they don't reach the people that matter."

Zan sipped her coffee thoughtfully. "So what can you do?"

"I need help. That's where the second condition comes in. I need you."

"Me?"

"As you also pointed out last night, your column *does* reach a lot of people. And here in San Francisco they're the right people, people who can do something. You could write a column on the plight of the women."

"Stu, I write a humor column. I can't write about this issue."

"It's important."

"I know that. But it's not the kind of thing I do."

Stu put his coffee cup down carefully. "So you'll write about silly single men pursuing romance in sushi bars while these women are being pushed out on the street. Can you justify that? You're a journalist, after all. You have a responsibility—"

"Stu," Zan broke in, trying to keep her voice low and even, "don't tell me what my responsibility is. Are you trying to corner the market on being self-righteous?"

Stu crossed the kitchen and put his cup in the sink. His movements were tight and controlled, his anger plainly simmering below the surface. She felt a despair totally out of proportion to the argument. She had been right. They couldn't get along, not even for five minutes.

Stu turned around and faced her. "You don't want to have an impact, to change people's minds?"

"Of course I do. I want to make them laugh at themselves. I want them to be a little nicer to each other. That's the best I can do."

"So you won't help me."

"I didn't say that. I'll help you. You want publicity, I'll figure out a way for you to get it. But I can't give you a muckraking column with facts and figures. It might have to be a different way."

"What will you do?"

"I haven't come up with a plan yet," Zan said impatiently. "It usually takes me more than three minutes. As soon as I do, you'll be the first to know."

Stu hesitated, then nodded rapidly in acceptance. "So we have a deal?"

"We have a deal."

He held out his hand for her to shake. She took it warily, afraid of touching him again. His palm was hard and callused, and his fingers took hers in a firm grip and didn't let go. He had kissed her, aroused her, rejected her, and insulted her. But his eyes were warm as he held her hand, and Zan felt herself melting all over again. She fought the loose dissolving feeling and straightened her shoulders. From now on, she decided, the trick in handling Stu Temple would be *no physical contact.* Not even handshakes. The man could turn the friendly custom into an intimate suggestive act. She'd keep her distance, and she'd be able to handle him just fine. Zan gently tugged her hand free and avoided his eyes.

Stu was fifteen minutes late. Zan banged her front gate behind her and considered hiking down to the waterfront. What if he had forgotten about her and gone straight to the shoot? When she'd called to tell him that her first "date" had been confirmed with Toby Jones, corporate lawyer and windsurfing champion, he'd offered her a ride in such an offhand way, hardly listening to her thanks, that it could have slipped his mind.

In the planning conferences they'd had with Mark McFee over the past two weeks Stu had often seemed distracted. She'd caught him glowering at her, his thoughts seemingly a million miles away. It was probably his irritation at wasting his time on an inconsequential piece of fluff.

Perhaps he was paying her back for being slow to respond to his request for publicity for the Paradise Perdue Home. Zan had dutifully read the research materials he'd supplied her with, but she still hadn't come up with an angle. She didn't want to write a dull obligatory piece that would sink without a trace. She wanted to show Stu that she could make a difference and accomplish something in her own way.

That was the galling thing, she admitted to herself. Her pride was at stake. Although she'd managed to keep her tone businesslike and reserved, she was slowly going mad being so near him. The stunning kiss in her kitchen still haunted her; the feverishness of her response still amazed her. But Stu was just as reserved as she, and not only that, he was vaguely patronizing about her work. So like a tomboy determined to climb a taller tree than the boy next door, she was fixed on beating him at his own game. It was childish, but she was sure the outcome would be very satisfying. Stu Temple cowed, his blue eyes gone from mocking to humble, taking her hand. *Zan, forgive me,* he'd say. *I never knew what a talent like yours could accomplish...*

A car horn bleated and Zan looked up, startled, to see Stu looking anything but humble.

"Wake up," he bellowed out the car window. "We're late."

"Who's fault is that?" she snapped back, leaning over to pick up her gear. "I've been waiting for you for fifteen minutes."

"It's our fault, Zan," a woman's voice called. "Don't blame dear Stu."

Dear Stu? Zan looked up. She noticed for the first time that Stu had three women crammed in the station wagon with the video equipment. They must be his friends from the Paradise Perdue Home for Retired Actresses. The one in the front seat with Stu waved at her, and they all nodded and smiled. They looked amiable and slightly giggly, and inordinately curious about her. Zan approached the car feeling like a prize heifer at a 4H judging. She stowed her gear in the back of the wagon and climbed into the middle seat with two of the women.

The woman next to her spoke first. She had curly light gray hair that sat on her head like a cap, and a pair of extraordinarily large, slightly slanted green eyes. Laugh lines radiated outward from the corners. She was still beautiful, Zan thought, and she must have been devastating when she was younger. No wonder she had become an actress. "I'm Alberta Granville," she said, "but please call me Bertie. This is Faye Foxe, and that's Amelia Marsh in front. We've heard all about you from Stu."

Faye removed an enormous pair of dark sunglasses to peer at Zan. She had short-cropped, jet-black hair and a trim figure in a pair of black pants and sweater. She crossed delicate feet with bright red toenails in wide-strapped black sandals. "We were the clever ones who sent Stu's tape to Just One Look. He was just adorable on it, wasn't he? And to think he actually met *you*. We're simply thrilled." Her voice was husky with what Zan imagined had to be whiskey and cigarettes, and had a trace of a British accent. "We *are* a bit late, but Stu took us out to brunch and we got to talking as we always do, and of course he couldn't get us to move until we finished the very last drop of champagne. You're very beautiful, dear, do you know that?" She patted Zan's knee familiarly. "Young and fresh. I can tell you haven't had great tragedy in your life, or a great love affair yet, but don't despair."

"Oh hush," Amelia spoke up from the front seat. "Don't be so dramatic all the time, Faye. You'd think you were still on a movie set." She patted her gray hair, pulled back in a bun, and finding it satisfactorily arranged, straightened the collar of her dress. "Don't mind her Zan, she has to inject drama into life or she calls it boring. She insisted on champagne this morning. Personally I prefer coffee, don't you?"

"Well, I . . ." Zan began confusedly, but Faye interrupted.

"Well of course we all like coffee, darling, it revs you up so nicely, but when you're shut up in that decaying monster of a house—not that it wasn't lovely at one time, or couldn't be again—with no money for theatre tickets or new clothes, well, I don't think you can afford to treat champagne for breakfast as if we were all going to hell in a hand-cart."

"Yes, but you see what happened," Bertie broke in, "after all we did make Stu late."

"Yes, but Zan doesn't mind, do you darling?"

Zan opened her mouth to respond but Amelia chimed in from the front seat, "Don't answer that, Zan. Honestly, Faye, you're always putting people in the most impossible positions."

"Oh, rot," Faye answered mulishly.

Throughout this extraordinary conversation Stu seemed to be concentrating on his driving, but Zan sneaked a look at him in the rearview mirror and noticed one corner of his mouth twitching suspiciously. Their eyes met for a moment and they smiled, sharing their mutual amusement. Zan felt a peculiar warmth at the brief bond between them.

"So you're going windsurfing, Zan," Bertie said. "How thrilling. Have you done it before?"

"Once, on a vacation in Hawaii. My instructor gave up and told me to go have a piña colada instead. I wasn't exactly a star pupil."

Bertie laughed. "It seems very difficult to me."

"All I can advise," Faye said, lighting a cigarette and blowing a cloud of smoke out of the window, "is to keep your knees bent and wear waterproof mascara."

Amelia turned around to join in the conversation. "I don't quite understand the fascination your generation has with certain things. Windsurfing—I'm sure it's exhilarating, but there you are out on the bay all alone and who can you show off to? Now we had tennis parties and sailing..."

"Water skiing."

"It all sounds fun," Zan said. "Sometimes I feel a little out of step with what's popular today."

"Oh yes, darling, we know. We read your column faithfully. So amusing, we were dying to meet you, and you turned out so satisfactorily," Faye said. "Well, there was croquet, you know..."

"Moonlight sails to Catalina," Bertie continued dreamily, then sat up and shook her head briskly. "But you mustn't think it was all roses, Zan, no indeed. Life is just easy when you're young, that's all."

"Oh, but I don't agree," Faye said. "It's dreadfully hard, all those crises one has to get through."

"It's the surviving that makes it so enjoyable in the end," Amelia concluded, and for once no one contradicted her.

Faye sighed and stubbed out her cigarette. "It's true. But surviving is so dreary these days, thanks to Paradise's awful son Dwayne. I never liked him. No money for anything, no going out. Of course we have Stu, he buys us these lovely champagne breakfasts and things, and he's so obligingly making this picture—excuse me, Stu, *film*—which is absolutely going to save our skins, but still, he is rather young and one longs for male companionship of the more romantic sort."

"Maybe you do." Amelia's voice was prim.

"Oh we all do, let's face it, we're not dead are we?"

Amelia and Bertie both opened their mouths but Stu broke in. "Here we are," he announced, pulling up in front of a dilapidated Victorian house with a sagging wraparound porch. "I'll see you all tomorrow. I'm shooting reminiscences with Tanya and Livie."

"What do they know?" Faye said. "You've already gotten your best stuff from us."

"You can be terribly nasty, Faye," Stu said, his eyes twinkling. "I think you'd get along well with Zan."

"I'm very sure I would, darling, we both have a critical turn of mind. We appreciate the finer things, you know." Faye got out and Amelia and Bertie followed.

"Goodbye, Zan," Bertie called. "Come and visit."

"Yes, please," Amelia echoed. "We'd love to see you."

"Do relieve us of this painful misery in our old age," Faye concluded, and they all waved and went up the walk, still talking.

Zan waved goodbye and slid into the front seat next to Stu. "I've never seen three women who were less old or less miserable."

"I know," Stu said, and they laughed together. He pulled away and headed along Sausalito harbor. A frown crossed his face as he continued, "Sometimes I'm afraid that they're looking at my film as the solution to all of their problems."

"Maybe they're saying that so you'll believe it too."

Stu looked startled, then thoughtful, a reaction to her statements Zan was getting used to. Then he smiled. "Maybe you're right. It would be just like them. I'm worried, though. Dwayne is coming back from Europe and I hear he's trying to get the city of Sausalito to evict them from the house."

"Do you think he can?"

"Who knows? The house is in deplorable shape. It's an eyesore, really, and the town depends on the tourist trade. That porch is going to fall in with the next heavy rain."

"Well, at least it's the end of August and the rainy season is still months away."

"I wish it were that simple. Time is running out." Stu glowered at the line of traffic in front of them.

Zan looked out at the bay and stared with unseeing eyes at the lush hills of Angel Island. Stu had an uncanny ability to confuse her. Her feelings were contradictory and turbulent, and she couldn't seem to sort them out. For the past two weeks she'd despised him for treating her project as a diversion or a joke, and now she only wanted to help him with his.

And now that she'd met Amelia, Bertie and Faye, she was more determined to help them than ever. They'd turned out so differently from what she'd expected; they were hardly the grandmotherly types she'd pictured hovering around Stu. Zan shook her head at her foolishness. She'd certainly never imagined them enjoying champagne brunches and yearning for romantic companionship...

Wait a minute. Zan closed her eyes for a moment and tried to concentrate. An idea was hovering around the edges of her mind, but it was too nebulous and slippery to grasp. But seeing the women in a new light had somehow pointed the way to help the Paradise Perdue Home, and the answer was right in front of her. If she could just get ahold of it...

"Worrying about staying up on that windsurfer? The bay looks pretty choppy today."

Zan tore her eyes away from the bay and looked over at Stu. "Oh, I'll be fine," she said distractedly. "Toby promised to teach me everything he knows."

Stu's half-smile turned into a glower, and Zan supposed he was thinking about the traffic again. She studied his profile and resolved to show him that she could be serious and have a sense of humor, too. Just wait until he saw what could be done with a touch of fun instead of gloom. She was a competent, mature professional, and she'd be damned if she'd let Stu Temple think of her as an insubstantial clown.

With a shriek of horrified surprise, Zan found herself sliding along the slick surface of the windsurfer, banging her shin on the sail, and tumbling headfirst into the icy cold water of San Francisco Bay. When she surfaced and pushed a clump of hair out of her eyes she met, once again, the unrelenting lens of Stu Temple's camera.

"Get away from me!" she roared, and waded back to the board. She clambered up on it like a camel, closing her eyes against the knowledge that she was offering a rather awkward view of her hindquarters. Stu had faithfully recorded her every clumsy move since she'd waded into the water; every time she turned around he was there, camera grinding, his large amused grin plainly visible behind it.

He'd had the nettlesome quality of a burr under a saddle ever since they'd pulled into Windy Sea Windsurfing. Their easy camaraderie in the car had evaporated with the appearance of Toby Jones, who had glided into the parking lot in a red Mercedes convertible, wearing an easy smile and hundred-dollar Italian sneakers, which Stu kept accidentally treading on all day.

Stu had reverted to his usual cranky professionalism for the shoot, but he'd worn a particularly black expression, even for him. He'd only seemed to cheer up briefly when Jack Frost, his assistant—"How're you doing, just please don't make fun of my name, okay?"—peeled into the parking lot and deposited a fine film of dust on the gleaming finish of Toby's car. Toby's smile had gotten rather strained as he told Jack not to worry about it, and it was only luck that prevented his seeing Stu's broad grin.

The atmosphere didn't improve during the taping. Toby turned out to be a curly headed dynamo, and they'd had a funny, fast-moving interview while he'd given her a lesson on the windsurfer on land. Or perhaps its fast-moving quality had to do with Stu's periodic growls at Toby to hurry up because the light was fading. Toby had insisted on concentrating on his demonstration of how to lean into the wind, however, despite Stu's impatience. Zan had just been getting the hang of it, leaning back with Toby holding on to her waist for balance, when Stu knocked over the sail with his camera, bonking Toby on the head.

Now Zan was fast approaching fury as she reached for the sail and resolved to stay on her feet this time. Stu was enjoying filming her humiliating performance way too much. She gritted her teeth and made her usual wobbly attempt to rise, but she lost her balance and fell with a gentle plop into the freezing bay.

That did it. Zan hooked her arm around the windsurfer and waded back to shore. Toby was still gliding out on the bay, oblivious to the waning sun. She could feel goosebumps underneath her wetsuit and her teeth chattered in a fast stacatto as she tried to lift the board out of the water. She succeeded only in pulling a muscle and drenching her deck shoes, which she'd left at the water's edge. She could see out of the corner of her eye that Stu was approaching, and she sighed in relief; at least help was on the way. "This thing must weigh a ton," she called, and turned to Stu to find him standing a few feet away, making no move to help her. In fact, he was calmly filming her exhausting struggle.

"You swine!" Zan dropped the windsurfer abruptly, took careful aim, and with a tremendous thrust sent a cascade of water splashing all over Stu and that omnipresent camera. Then, with a final heroic effort, she hauled the contraption out of the bay and dropped it on the beach.

"I have that on tape, you know," Stu said, laughter bubbling underneath his words. Zan ignored him and stalked up the sand to her towel. She collapsed on it wearily and tilted her face to catch the weakening rays of the sun.

She opened one eye when Stu flopped down beside her. Zan watched as a bead of water dropped off a dark eyelash and hit his cheek. She followed its path through the slight stubble, all the way down to the full mouth. Stu's tongue flicked out, caught the drop and disappeared. Zan found her whole attention focused on that sensuous, beautiful mouth.

"Salty," Stu remarked, grinning. The sun and wind had brought color to his cheeks and made his eyes seem even bluer. Even the sea and the sky were no competition for those eyes, Zan reflected. Then she remembered that she was furious with him.

She raised herself up on her elbows. "Did you have to capture every second of my humiliation on that blasted thing? What am I, comic relief?"

"Just doing my job. Where'd you learn to splash like that? I'm soaked."

"Combine me, my older brother, and Blue Spring Lake every summer vacation and you'll get the answer."

"You have a brother?"

Zan looked out at the bay, where Toby was expertly maneuvering his way back to shore. "You should get some shots of Toby."

"Jack is doing it. What about—"

"I'd better change or I'll catch pneumonia. At least I know that if I do, you'll be around to film it." Zan rose, slung her towel around her neck, and headed for the dressing room.

Even the change into dry clothes didn't warm her chilled bones. Zan hesitated as she brushed out her hair, which was drying into its usual soft waves. She'd been annoyed with Stu all afternoon, but she knew that her reluctance to leave the dressing room and face him again had more to do with the feelings he'd aroused. His proximity had unnerved her in a far more subtle and dangerous way than her surface irritation. She gripped her hairbrush, hard, and wondered when this reaction to Stu would slow, and cease. It had to. After all, she had to work with the man.

She gave her hair a final vigorous brush and left the dressing room. Fog was now barreling through the Golden Gate in a great gray mass and only the tops of the bridge towers were visible. Zan shivered; the weather in the Bay Area could change drastically in a matter of minutes, and the temperature seemed to have dropped twenty degrees since she'd been on the bay.

"This is the kind of weather that calls for brandy and a fire."

Zan turned to see Toby Jones behind her. He had changed into dry clothes as well, and his blond hair was drying in crisp tight curls around his tanned face. He was fastening his heavy gold watch to his wrist and frowning in concentration. Zan realized idly that it was the first time she'd seen him without his smile all day.

Toby looked up and the ever-present smile resurfaced. "Sorry about deserting you out there on the bay, but when the wind starts to blow I have a tendency to get carried away."

"Literally or figuratively?"

"What? Oh, yes, I see what you mean, that's rather clever. Both, I guess. So what do you say to my spiriting you away to a nice warm Sausalito bar?"

Zan hesitated. Suddenly Toby's wholesome, bland good-natured appeal seemed exactly what she needed. She needed to relax in its safe confines, not in the tangled web of a darkly moody Irishman with a penchant for wicked behavior and a delight in making her uncomfortable. "Sounds wonderful," she said.

"Brandy and a fire, coming up."

Zan reached down for her bag but found a familiar strong hand had already gripped it. "Yes, that does sound nice," Stu said easily. "It's a pity Zan can't join you. She has to come with me."

Zan gaped at him. "What are you talking about?"

"We have to look at the footage we shot today. It's easier if we catalog it as we go along, and I need you to do that. You'll be editing it with me, so you'll have to be around." He turned to Toby. "You understand, work comes first."

"Oh, of course. See you, then. Let me know when the piece airs." Toby walked away with a carelessness Zan found somewhat damaging to her ego. She turned to Stu furiously.

"Just what do you think you're doing? You can't order me around!"

Stu took her arm and began to walk toward his station wagon. "I'm not ordering you around," he said in a reasonable tone, "but I am the producer, and I do have more experience than you, and I know that doing things this way will be better for us in the long run. If you look at what you shoot as you go along..."

"I'm not arguing with that, I'm saying that I don't have to look at it at your convenience!"

They stopped by the car and Stu dropped her arm. He waved goodbye to Jack Frost absently, then cocked his head to one side and looked at her. "I'm sorry I scared away your date."

"It wasn't a date, for heaven's sake, but I'm exhausted and freezing."

"I can offer you brandy and a fire too. And a video monitor. What else could you ask for?"

"Where might that be?" Zan asked, but she already knew the answer; her pounding pulse told her.

"At my house." Stu's eyes were unreadable, but his tone was offhand. He reached out to circle her wrist with his fingers and he gave it a slight tug. "It'll be warmer and pleasanter than my office. And it's closer. Strictly professional, of course." He dropped her wrist.

"Of course." Zan's mouth was dry. Stu's innocent touch had disturbed her and she tried to organize her thoughts but failed miserably. When he inclined his head toward the car she got in without thinking. It was only when he slid in on the opposite side and turned on the engine that she began to panic. What was she doing? A foggy evening, a fire, brandy, and Stu Temple were definitely a dangerous combination. As he pulled out of the parking lot Zan cast a backward despairing glance at the windsurfer on the beach and wondered if she could escape from the car and leap on it. Would it somehow carry her away across the bay without dumping her into it again?

"I'll have you warmed up in five minutes." Stu's voice broke into her thoughts, making her jump.

"Five minutes? You must live near the water."

"I live *on* the water. You'll see."

Stu fell silent and concentrated on his driving. The fog was now heavy and thick, swirling around the car in a fine white mist. It completely obscured the city across the bay, and trailed in long fingers down the hills. Zan should have been grateful for the chance to collect her thoughts, but she found herself longing for some inconsequential chatter. This silence wasn't benign; it was as dense as the fog outside her window, thick with things unspoken.

She was relieved when Stu pulled into a parking lot. Bobbing out on the water was the bizarre collection of houseboats that were as much a part of Sausalito as the art galleries downtown. They weren't ordinary houseboats; they were rather a fantastic, friendly floating village of oddly shaped wooden houses that happened to be on water. Somehow she'd never expected that Stu would live in such a whimsical place.

He pulled into a space and shut off the engine. When Zan didn't move he reached over and touched her hand briefly. "Zan—" Stu stopped abruptly and felt her hand again. "Your hand is freezing. And you're still trembling."

She was trembling from more than the cold, but she couldn't tell him that. "Maybe I should get home," she said, her voice slightly shaky. "We could do this tomorrow."

She looked over at Stu and their eyes caught and held in that same time-stopping gaze that had occurred in the bar when they'd met, and she could read Stu's desire as plainly as she had that night. He raised her fingers to his mouth. "So cold," he murmured. He teased her fingertips with his lips, then drew them softly into his mouth. Zan gasped at the shock of the moist warm sweetness as he gently ran his tongue over the sensitive pads, then nipped at them slightly with his teeth. He turned her hand over and gently kissed her palm.

Zan looked at Stu's mouth on her skin and knew then with absolute certainty that it was impossible to battle her attraction any more. It was a pounding, powerful force and she had no experience with fighting such a sensation. She had never felt this before, this mindless, heedless, dizzying rush into a sensuality that shocked her with its wild, irresistible core. She wanted to touch him, taste him, smell him, capture him and make him her own.

She saw Stu read her desire in her gaze and his eyes turned a smoky cobalt. He pulled her to him with a strength she found impossible to resist and his mouth burned against hers when he kissed her. Her head thrown back, she drank in the taste of him. Here was the unchecked power they had hesitated to explore in her kitchen, and it was so heady and dangerous she knew why she'd been afraid of it.

Stu withdrew slightly and reached for her hand again. "Warmer now?"

"Yes," Zan whispered, and as Stu bent to seek the softness of her neck she whispered "yes," again. His lips were warm and sweet and moved softly against her. They trailed down her shoulder as he slid the loose neck of her sweater down to bare it, and "yes," she whispered again. He followed the length of her arm to the pulse at the inside of her elbow and lingered there to breathe in her scent. "Oh yes," she murmured. She no longer knew what she was saying, the word was a litany of her willingness and her surrender, and when Stu lifted his head to fix her with his probing glance she knew the answer to the question on his lips before he asked it.

"Will you come inside with me now?"

"Yes," she said.

Chapter Four

They walked in silence down the dock. Zan felt borne along by Stu and the force of her desire, as though in a dream, so heedless to the outside world did she feel. Hand in hand with Stu she walked through a neighborhood whose sidewalks undulated with the gentle rhythm of the sea, where the air had a salty fresh tang and was filled with the sounds of sea gulls crying the passing of the day.

Stu turned off the main dock and led her along a smaller one, all the way to the end, where he stopped in front of the last houseboat, a strange wooden structure with odd angles that gave it a slightly off-kilter appearance. It wasn't until Zan followed the clean lines of wood and glass that she saw its unique unstudied elegance and grace. They stepped onto the wide porch and he dug into his pocket for his keys with one hand, still holding her hand with the other.

He continued to hold it as he pushed open the door and inclined his head for her to enter. Zan stepped through the door expecting to find a small cramped area but saw instead a large living space with windows that embraced the sweep of the bay and a skylight that flooded the room with the soft gray light of the waning afternoon. Sleek modern lamps perched like black birds among a scattering of antique furniture, and an invitingly overstuffed rose-colored couch sat in front of the fireplace.

"I promised you a fire." Stu's voice was soft but it made her jump; they hadn't exchanged a word since they'd left the car.

"And a videotape monitor," she reminded him weakly. They crossed the room together, and as Stu bent down to light the already laid fire she sank down on the couch, nervous for the first time since she'd agreed to come in.

She examined Stu as he leaned forward to urge the flames. The dancing light was having an extraordinary effect on his jet-black hair, giving it a burnished tinge. It softened the lines of his face as well, and his full lower lip looked tender and welcoming. Zan snuggled deeper into the couch and extended her cold feet toward the fire. She felt enormously content just to watch Stu in the firelight while the heat he had aroused in her body remained, now dormant but giving her a small thrill of expectation.

Stu gave the logs a last poke and leaned back against the couch, placing his hand casually on her foot. He felt it more carefully, then looked up at her quickly. "Your shoes are soaking wet."

"I know. I kind of splashed them when I landed back on the beach."

"Don't move." Stu got up and headed out of the room, returning a moment later with a glass of brandy. Handing it to her silently, he headed out again. Zan sipped it gratefully and he reappeared shortly with a basin of steaming water.

"Stu, I'm fine," she insisted, though she was still cold. "The fire is already warming me up."

Stu didn't reply; he sat down at her feet and began to remove her shoes.

"Stu, you don't have to—"

"Shut up," he interrupted in a polite tone and rolled up her black corduroys to her calves.

Zan took another sip of brandy. For the first time in her life, she wished she was the type of woman who got pedicures. Her feet were perfectly okay, she knew, smooth and rather small, but if a gorgeous man like Stu Temple was fondling them, as he was at that moment, shouldn't she at least have a slash of Ravishing Red on the nails?

Stu gently slipped her feet into the steaming water. Despite her nervousness, Zan let out a sigh of pure pleasure and leaned her head back on the sofa. Tension seemed to leave her whole body and she wiggled her toes appreciatively. "That feels wonderful."

Stu rolled up the sleeves of his soft blue shirt to the elbows and slipped his hands inside the basin. Then he rubbed her arch gently, first one foot, then the other. He gazed up into her face, flushed from the fire and the brandy, and looked down again. "You are so lovely," he said to her feet. His wet fingers trailed up and circled her ankle.

Zan looked down at Stu's bent head. She felt lost, swept away into another world, a floating world with the sound of water lapping and sea gulls crying and the occasional mournful sigh of a foghorn, with the air suffused with soft gray twilight and the red-gold glow of the fire. But all of that beauty, the sound and light and color, was merely a backdrop to the man below her. He was what made up this new world, and his piercing eyes and strong hands were what held her there, willingly entrapped. Tantalizing new territory beckoned, and she was the breathless pioneer.

Stu leaned over and kissed away the drops of water he'd left on her ankle. "Warm socks," he said.

Zan made an effort to go from the transcendent to the practical. "What?"

He rose athletically and headed for the bedroom. "You need a towel and some warm socks."

She sipped her brandy, glad she had a moment alone to collect herself. She'd almost gone off her rocker there for a moment. What was she doing rhapsodizing about Stu Temple? Tantalizing territory, indeed. She wasn't a poet, she was a satirist, and she'd better remember it. Zan placed her glass back on the table decisively as a small towel came flying across the room and hit her on the head. A pair of red wool socks soon followed.

"Towel yourself off and get outfitted, woman."

Zan bent down obediently and dried off her feet, then put on the thick pair of socks. She padded across the living area in the direction Stu's voice had come from and found him in a small airy kitchen, pouring himself a glass of brandy.

He looked up. "Warmer now?"

"Toasty."

"Good." Stu put the brandy bottle back in the cupboard and grabbed her hand firmly. "Back to the couch."

"What a nice kitchen." Zan pulled away and inched along the counter. She'd seen that look in Stu's eyes before, and she suddenly felt the need to stall. "Nice cabinets. You keep them well stocked, too...wait, I can't believe this. Oreos, chocolate-chip, *and* Mallomars? And fudge-nut? Have a bit of a sweet tooth?"

"I keep them for guests."

"Are you friends with an army of ten-year-olds?"

"All right, I confess—I'm a hopeless chocoholic. You should taste my homemade chocolate-chip cookies. Now let's go back to the couch."

Zan neatly evaded his arm and stood on tiptoe to peer toward the back of the shelf. "Are you solely responsible for the funding of the Girl Scouts of America? There must be twenty boxes back there. Hmm . . . it's a wonder you manage to look so—" She had difficulty catching her breath when she felt Stu move up behind her. When she eased back on her heels she bumped into him, her bottom pressed snugly against him. Stu put his arms around her waist and settled her there more firmly.

Zan cleared her throat. "So you bake cookies, huh? I'm impressed."

"I'm glad." Stu's broad hand stroked her stomach lazily and his breath stirred the hair by her ear. "I'm told I'm very good at it, too." He slid his hand underneath her loose cotton sweater and rested it against her skin.

"I'm sure you are," Zan said faintly.

"The secret is concentration," Stu went on, his voice low. His lips brushed softly against her neck. "And, of course, the right ingredients." His tongue trailed up toward her ear. "Sweetness and spice. And then—"

"And then?" Zan asked breathlessly as she felt his teeth lightly scrape the outside of her ear.

"A very hot oven." Stu turned her around to face him and his mouth descended on hers. He gave a small groan deep in his throat as she met his lips with a sizzling heat that surprised her as much as him. She was teetering near the edge of her control, and she couldn't stand being teased by his whispering touch any longer. All she wanted was the full force of him.

Stu cupped her face in his hands as he deepened the kiss until all sound, all thought of anything but him simply disappeared. Then his hands slid underneath her sweater again, his fingers encircling her waist for a brief instant, tracing its curve, before sweeping up to caress her breasts through her silk camisole. Zan swayed as heat spread up to her face and made her dizzy. She gripped Stu's shoulders as his mouth descended to where his hands had been.

He kissed her there, then slid her sweater over her head in one easy movement and brought her back against him. She was now wearing only her camisole, but the soft cotton of his shirt was too much of a barrier between them. She tried to unbutton it as he kissed her again, but as she tugged at it, she felt Stu shake with suppressed laughter.

"Don't laugh," she said sternly, and Stu stopped obediently. They grinned at each other before Zan bent again to concentrate on her task. With unsteady fingers she undid the buttons and the shirt slipped to the floor. She ran her hands lovingly over his chest, then slowly followed the small trail of hair down toward the waistband of his jeans.

"Zan," Stu said in a choked voice.

She paused and looked up at him. She'd been so immersed in the feel of his bare skin that she hadn't thought of his response, or of how far she was leading them. Now she was fully aware of how much he wanted her, and his eyes were darkly blue and serious as he met her uncertain look.

"Don't stop," Stu said huskily. "Don't ever stop." He brought her hand back to his chest and held it against the swift beating of his heart.

His words and the feel of his heartbeat sent a tremor through her, and when Stu captured her lips again in a hungry kiss she didn't resist. She could feel the strength of his response through his jeans, and she could not pull back. He drew her entire length against him, and the textures of skin and denim and the roughness of his hair against her were her only reality. It was a new self she had discovered, a ravenous, voracious self, and she ran her hands down his back in a fierce caress to bring him even closer to her.

Now she weaved unsteadily with the force of his embrace, and Stu slowly lowered himself to the floor, bringing her along with him until she was stretched out on top of him, nestled in his arms. Their mouths stayed together in a deep kiss that seemed to go on forever. When they finally drew apart, they looked into each other's eyes, shaken.

Stu took a deep breath and let it out slowly. "Hello there," he said softly.

"Hi."

"Much as I'm enjoying this, the kitchen floor isn't exactly the most romantic spot. What do you say we try the bedroom instead?"

The bedroom. If she agreed, there would be no turning back, Zan knew. But the posing of the question had opened up the possibility of choice; she could not continue to be merely swept away, without thought, on Stu's kitchen floor. And she knew, looking into Stu's grave eyes, that that was the reason he had stopped them to ask. She knew without him telling her that he wanted her to make a conscious decision, to be sure.

She *wasn't* sure, but it was hard to think while lying on about six foot three inches of disturbing masculinity. She would have to be very strong to resist this temptation, she knew. Stu's fingers lightly brushed her breast, back and forth, back and . . . Zan decided to stall. "Shouldn't we screen the tapes from today?" she asked, a teasing note in her voice. "I do remember someone saying that work does come first, so—"

Stu nibbled on her neck. "I wouldn't exactly call that work."

Zan froze as he moved on to her ear. The hazy warm buzz of sensuality was replaced by a needle of sharp awareness. Stu had done it again. Once again he'd made a casual comment trivializing her work, downplaying its importance. And she'd been only a whisper away from following him into his bedroom and making love to him with every particle of passion she possessed. She'd almost forgotten everything she knew about herself and given herself to a man who didn't know her, couldn't ever know her, because she *was* her work and he would never value it.

And she knew that walking into the bedroom, for her, would have been no insignificant act. She was a modern woman; she observed and reported on her times. But when she measured herself against them, she saw that she was often out of step. She had never been the possessor of a casual heart. Letting Stu make love to her would be a mistake, a foolish glimpse into an intimacy she could never share with him. He would know one side of her and none of the other, so the gift of that knowledge would mean nothing. They would have a particular kind of closeness, but with a core of loneliness and loss.

Stu lifted his head from her neck at her long silence, waiting for her response.

"I'm sorry, Stu. I can't make love to you."

His eyes were strangely watchful, quiet. "You can't?"

Sighing, she eased herself off him and shivered at the chill air against her bare shoulders. She looked around for her sweater and Stu handed it to her gently. She pulled it on and stood up. "I'm sorry I let it go this far. But I think we should stick to what we decided in my kitchen—strictly business. We should stay away from physical involvement."

"Or maybe we should just stay away from kitchens." Stu got up slowly and reached for his shirt. Zan watched as he buttoned it and the beautiful chest she'd ran her trembling fingers over disappeared. She felt a pang of regret that had nothing to do with her better sense, and it convinced her she was doing the right thing. Pangs of any kind were to be avoided at all costs.

"All things considered, I think it would be better if we looked at tapes in your office from now on," she said carefully. "Can you give me a lift home now?"

"Of course." The unreadable look was in Stu's eyes again. Zan followed him listlessly back to the living area, feeling drained.

She slipped back into her shoes and walked silently beside him to the car, telling herself that the misery she felt would quickly pass. It was just that being next to him was so difficult. The touch of his hand on her elbow as he guided her into the car was electric. She slid into the seat and stared straight ahead as he drove, trying to think of the things that made her happy, that made her Alexandra Adelaide Flanders, not the wild wanton who had just rolled about on some strange man's linoleum. Her work. Her house. Peanut butter and jelly sandwiches. Chili dogs. Cary Grant movies. Champagne. Hot baths. Kissing Stu...

She'd better go back to the beginning. Her work. That was what was important. It was also the key to concentrating on something other than Stu, as well as the key to having him respect her. The two goals might seem contradictory, but they actually weren't, Zan told herself firmly. The way to forget Stu was to remember what a patronizing oaf he really was.

And to beat him at his own game. Zan mused again on the idea that had been tickling her brain this afternoon about the Perdue Home. It had something to do with how vibrant Amelia, Bertie and Faye had been, but there was more. She remembered Amelia's puzzlement about modern pastimes—"There you are out on the bay all alone and who can you show off to?"—and the way their voices had brightened when they'd described their amusements in Hollywood. And finally Faye's bluntness, saying that they all still wanted romantic companionship, they weren't dead, were they?

Zan sat up with a start as Stu turned onto her street. That was it. It was rather an unorthodox way to rally support for the women, but it could work. Now all she had to do was clear it with Mark McFee, then call Amelia, Bertie and Faye...and Stu? Zan shot a quick look at him while he pulled up in front of her house. Those eyebrows and that grim mouth looked too threatening to deal with at the moment. She should clear it with the other parties first, anyway. She couldn't wait to run inside and call Mark.

She turned to smile at Stu, her hand on the door. "Good night. I'll talk to you on Monday about screening those tapes, okay?" Stu nodded stiffly and she got out, then leaned back in the window. "Oh yes—thanks for the lift today. Bye."

Stu nodded again, and she ran up the path to the front door. Her eagerness to get inside and start the ball rolling was tempered by a tiny strain of annoyance at Stu. A man should at least be cordial, even if a woman had refused his advances. The station wagon took off with a squeal of tires and Zan paused and looked back at the rapidly disappearing taillights. There was no question about it; she was dealing with a very touchy individual.

"When you said you'd bring lunch over, darling, we were expecting some corned beef sandwiches perhaps." Faye opened the door and eyed the two overstuffed shopping bags in Zan's arms. "Who's joining us this afternoon, the Third Battalion? Now wait a second, *there's* an idea..."

Zan groaned and set the bags down on the porch. "It's this problem I have with those gourmet delicatessens. I'm like a shark in a feeding frenzy. It was horrifying."

Bertie peered into the bags. "Whatever did you buy?"

"I don't remember everything, but I do seem to recall lobster salad, asparagus vinegrette, tomatoes with fresh basil, cold roast chicken, and proscuitto with melon."

"Oh dear. Well, let's eat it out here on the porch, where it's cool."

"Plus some kind of celery root thing with mustard dill sauce, artichoke heart salad, pasta salad, sourdough bread, an avocado, and two kinds of cheese. Oh, and some raspberries and a chocolate mousse torte." The three women gaped at her, and she added lamely, "Well, I thought maybe the other ladies might want some, too."

Amelia, Bertie and Faye stared at the bags. "Well," Faye finally said, "let's just hope the porch doesn't cave in."

While Amelia and Bertie set up a table in the shade, Zan and Faye dragged in a large cooler to keep the lemonade and imported beer cold. An unexpected heat wave had sent the usually moderate Bay Area temperatures soaring, and the women had all dressed in their coolest and loosest fitting clothes. Bertie looked around and smiled. "We all look so cool and lovely in these pale colors, like an Edwardian picnic. Especially Zan, with her hair up like that. Doesn't she look beautiful?"

"Striking," Faye agreed, then appraised Zan's ankle-length bare white dress. "Although you should show your legs a bit, darling. Men like that sort of thing, you know."

"She's perfect," Amelia said stoutly. "She's sexy without trying to be, which is something *some* of us might not be able to understand—"

"Oh, and I suppose you mean me?" Faye sniffed. "For your information, I made a *career* out of being sexy, Amelia, so I'm well qualified to—"

"Your career as a siren, you mean? Are we talking about on screen or off?"

Faye opened her mouth but Bertie stuck a piece of sourdough bread in it. "It's too hot to fuss, don't you think?" she asked brightly. "Amelia, help me bring in some of this food to the rest of the ladies. Faye, why don't you pour Zan a nice cold glass of lemonade."

Faye raised her eyebrows at Amelia's retreating back and poured two tall glasses of beer. She handed one to Zan. "All the ladies are in the den. One of Livie's old movies is on TV this afternoon and she's talked everyone into watching it." She leaned closer. "She plays a maid in the picture—has about ten lines of dialogue, but of course it's a *pivotal* part, you know. It's the *way* she says 'More tea, madam?' and 'Can I help you, sir?' They're all settled in there like she's doing Lady Macbeth."

"Don't listen to her," Bertie scolded as she came back on the porch. "She's the one who sent all those letters under assumed names to Channel Six asking them to run the movie. She knows how much it means to Livie."

Faye reached for her huge sunglasses and put them on. "Be quiet, Bertie, I'm trying to be caustic. Why don't you pass the roast chicken and let's eat. Now Zan, we're all ready to hear why you came over in this dreadfully hot weather to talk to us, though of course we're all agreed that you're charmingly dressed for it."

"I had an idea that I want to bounce off the three of you," Zan began as she helped herself to the chicken and passed it to Amelia. "Did Stu tell you about the series we're doing for 'Modern Times on Screen'?"

"Oh yes, all those dates with bachelors, he thinks it's very amusing."

"*Does* he?"

"He gave you such a lovely compliment, said that working with you isn't really like working at all. Isn't Stu a darling?"

"A positive treasure," Zan said grimly. She took a savage bite of chicken. "Anyway, do you remember those fake videodating tapes you all did on Stu's birthday? He said that each of you had made a tape, right?"

"Oh yes, dear. Try the asparagus, Bertie, it's delicious." Amelia passed the plate across the table.

"I think I might want to use them. Do you still have them? Are they any good?"

"Of course they're good," Faye said, "they're simply marvelous, and I'm wearing this divine purple dress. Oh

Amelia, I'm dying for that lobster salad, can you pass it—oh, thank you darling."

"Do you still have them?"

"Of course. Stu gave them to us, but it's silly. We don't have a VCR, but we think he might be getting us one," Bertie said fondly. "He is so sweet. Here, Amelia, you know how much you like celery root."

"Well, what I want to do is—"

"What is it in the lobster salad—basil?"

"Tarragon."

"I want to—"

"No, I think it's basil, Faye."

"Take the tapes and—"

"Tarragon," Faye said with finality. "Don't you agree, Zan, it couldn't possibly be anything else. Basil! Really."

Zan took a deep breath and said quickly, "I want to show each of your tapes on the show and have single men write in if they're interested in you."

The three women simultaneously swallowed and put down their forks.

"No!"

"You can't be serious!"

"Now that *is* marvelous news, I must say."

Zan nonchalantly took a bite of lobster salad, swallowed and nodded. "Tarragon."

"How *can* you talk of food?" Faye demanded. "Tell us everything immediately."

"I'd like to show one tape a week. If all goes well, we'll get some responses from gentlemen who are interested in each of you—it'll be like a videodating service, but the whole city will watch the tapes. You'll screen out the responses and pick your favorite."

"You're going to all this trouble to find us dates?" Bertie asked doubtfully.

"Yes, very sporting of you, Zan," Faye commented. "But why?"

"Because it's going to help save the Home. Here's my plan—each week one of you will go out on my 'date' with me, with Stu filming it. We'll go on one modern date—like a new wave dance club—and one 'old-fashioned' date—like, I don't know, a nightclub with big band music. You can help me come up with things to do. The interviews will be about whether things are more difficult for singles in the eighties—are people more protective of themselves? More selective? More self-absorbed? Unwilling to commit?"

"Sounds like it could be fun," Bertie said.

"And by the end of the series, the three of you will be kind of local celebrities. That's when we deliver the final punch."

"What's that, dear?"

"I haven't worked out all the details yet, but somehow we'll find a dramatic way to tell the audience about what's been happening at the Perdue Home. By then you won't be faceless 'retired actresses' anymore—you'll be Amelia, Bertie and Faye, who've been in the audience's living room every week. People will know you and like you and not want to see you get pushed around. What do you say?"

They looked at one another briefly, then turned to Zan and smiled.

"We say yes," Bertie announced. "Of course. What do we have to lose?"

"But enough of these trivial matters," Faye said airily. "Let's get to the really important issues. Whatever are we going to wear?"

was obvious that she was totally incapable of coherent thought; she couldn't even look at Stu without remembering their intimacies of the night before. She found herself looking at his hands and remembering them on her skin, and excitement and embarrassment rocked her so strongly she could barely see for a moment.

"So where is everybody else?" Stu asked. "Are they all watching Livie's movie?"

"They're glued to the screen," Amelia said. "Though I don't think they're following the plot. Livie shushes them whenever she comes on screen, but mostly they're just drinking beer and reminiscing."

A burst of laughter came through the open window. "You're not tempted to join them?" Stu asked.

"The stories are enchanting, but we've heard them all quite a few times already," Faye answered. "Besides, we were having too good of a time out here by ourselves. Being frivolous, you know." The four of them looked at one another and laughter bubbled out, soon turning into helpless giggles.

Stu looked around at the four of them, further fueling their amusement. "You all seem to have hit it off," he said gruffly.

"Best of friends already," Amelia said.

"We love her," Bertie chimed in.

"Absolutely," Faye said.

Stu stared off into the distance, squinting at the bay and looking disagreeable. Zan studied his profile and wondered if he was feeling a little left out. He seemed annoyed by her sudden friendship with the women. Maybe he did have feelings, after all. She should be nice to him, she supposed.

Another explosion of titters came from the den window and Zan turned to him. "Maybe we shouldn't have brought in that extra six-pack."

"Maybe."

"You know, I would think that you'd want to shoot the scene in there for your documentary. All the women watching an old movie that one of them has made—it has everything. Loyalty, affection, amusement, memories, laughter—"

"Quarreling, jealousy," Faye put in.

"Everything," Zan concluded. "Maybe you should have brought your camera over. Don't you think?"

"I think," Stu said evenly, putting his glass carefully on the table, "that you should let me decide how to make my film."

"Touchy, touchy. Of course, they're all laughing, not crying, so the scene can't be very important, right? Not that I'm qualified to have an opinion, of course."

"Maybe you should stick to your own field of expertise. Like, for instance, the new etiquette for singles bars. Don't ask him about the down payment on his condo until *after* you exchange numbers, and if he starts eyeing the blonde by the cappuccino machine quickly ask him about his stereo system and you'll have his attention for at least another hour. Very heavy stuff. I'm on pins and needles waiting for a column on tips for men."

"You'll need them. Most women don't respond well to grunts. Though, of course, the type *you'd* be interested in—"

"The thing is," Stu broke in calmly, "when I think of all the tiring, difficult research you had to do..." He shrugged. "Well, what can I say. I'm just filled with admiration."

"How about another beer, Stu?" Bertie broke in with false cheer.

Zan tore her furious gaze away from Stu and looked out stonily at the bay. That's what you get for trying to be nice to a spitting puma, she told herself. Remember to keep your distance next time.

"No thanks, Bertie, I have to be going. Just dropped by to say hello. Thanks for the cold beer." Stu stood up.

"Zan brought it," Amelia pointed out.

"Thanks to you then, Zan," Stu said stiffly.

Zan nodded shortly. She watched Stu go down the steps and climb into his station wagon and thought about how much she hated him. How could she have kissed him, how could she have clung to him like the simpering, mindless fool she was?

Faye heaved a long sigh and lit a cigarette. "The temperature seems to have risen several degrees out here. Whatever is going on with you and Stu?"

"Nothing. We just can't stand each other, that's all."

Amelia raised her eyebrows. "There did seem to be hostility there, but I'm not sure that's the cause."

Faye nodded. "Funny. I've never seen Stu so rude before. You really do provoke him. Interesting."

"You can both stop the innuendos," Zan said. "There's nothing going on, and there never will be. I think he's a patronizing boor, and he thinks—well, let's put it this way. The day I walk into Stu Temple's office as a war correspondent for the *New York Times*, wearing camouflage and holding a plane ticket to some war-torn country is the day he might begin to take me seriously. Until then, I don't think he thinks about me at all."

"You're forgetting one tiny thing," Bertie said. "Stu has never picked up a copy of *Modern Times* in his life."

"But that just proves my point, Bertie—"

"I don't think so, dear." When Zan looked at her questioningly, Bertie smiled gently. "He did this week. He read your column, didn't he?"

That stopped Zan, but only for a moment. "Only for ammunition," she said. "The battle lines have been drawn and we've only started the hostilities."

"You've started *something*, that's for certain," Faye said decidedly. "Now Zan, what do you say we dig into that divine mousse you brought. If you're going to forgo love, you might as well have chocolate."

Chapter Five

I know that I keep telling you this," Mark said as he stuck his head into Zan's office, "but we only have a five-day work week here. What are you doing here on a beautiful Saturday afternoon?"

"Mark, look at these." Zan waved a stack of letters in the air. "They're responses to last night's broadcast of Bertie's tape. Can you believe it? Hand-delivered, and the answering service says that they've already had about fifty calls."

Mark ambled in and leafed through a few of the letters and photographs. "Look at these guys—they're in better shape than I am. Who's this one, Cary Grant? You know, maybe this idea of yours wasn't so bad after all."

"You sure have a knack for praising your employees."

"I do my best. Listen, I have to get back to my office. Stop by later if you want to destroy some furniture, okay?"

"Sure." Zan returned her attention to the letters. Bertie was meeting her here for lunch along with Amelia and Faye, and she couldn't wait to see their reactions.

Bertie had called the night before after the broadcast, bubbling over with excitement. Zan had been half-afraid to pick up the receiver, certain it was Stu. She was still nervous when she thought about his possible reactions. It had been a relief to slip back into their cool professional mode this past week, and she didn't want to upset the delicate equilibrium with any more volatile emotions. She had a sinking feeling that Stu wouldn't exactly be an enthusiastic supporter of the plan.

Sighing, she rose from the desk and went to lay down on the floor of her office, her favorite posture when she was trying to think. How was she going to tell Stu what they'd done without making him furious? Why should she care? She toyed with several approaches but after five minutes came up only with the conclusion that her ceiling needed painting.

Her door opened abruptly. Zan gazed up a pair of familiar legs in faded jeans. She slowly trailed her eyes up past an unraveling gold sweater, over broad shoulders, a stubbled determined chin, and into a pair of furious blue eyes. Zan decided that she no longer needed to worry about how to tell Stu about her idea.

"Hi," she said, looking up at him. He was standing directly over her head, and the angle made him seem even taller, and a bit menacing.

"What are you doing on the floor?"

"I'm resting."

"I guess you must need it after all your secret machinations. Will you please get up, I can't yell at you properly if you're on the floor."

Zan got up and nervously crossed the room to get the desk between her and Stu. "What took you so long to come and yell?"

"I taped the show last night. Just saw it this morning." Stu began to pace. "What's going on in that head of yours? You're trying to find *dates* for Bertie?" He spun around to face her. "Is this your idea of a great plan? Didn't you say that as soon as you came up with one, I'd be the first to know?"

"Did I say that?"

"Why didn't you clear it with me first? I should have known you'd turn a desperate situation into an occasion for a party. I'm making a film about a terrible injustice being done to women who don't have the resources to fight back, and you turn the situation into a Noel Coward comedy! I turn the TV on and see Bertie giggling into a glass of champagne, talking about moonlight and roses—"

"What's wrong with that? Bertie's a woman, Stu. She's not a subject for a documentary or a case study. I have to help them the best way I know how. This is it."

"Do you mind informing me exactly how this plan of yours is going to accomplish that?"

Zan held up a stack of letters and shook them at Stu. "I'm turning them into *people*, Stu. People that the audience will follow for weeks, will start to care about and laugh with. Then when they hear about the Paradise Perdue Home for Retired Actresses they won't yawn and change the channel."

"You're trivializing the issue."

"I'm humanizing the issue. If you'd stop patronizing me for a moment, you'd realize that Amelia, Bertie and Faye *do* have the resources to fight back. They're actresses, Stu. They're attractive and bright and funny and comfortable in front of a camera. And they blow any stereotypes or prejudices about older women right out of the water. They can save themselves if we give them the chance. What's the matter? Are you afraid that you won't be their savior? Are you really thinking of them or are you trying to prove a point?"

Stu stared at her, his face drained of color, and Zan backpedaled hastily, afraid she'd gone too far. "I know you care about them. But if you'd just try to look at it from a different perspective..."

"The Zan Flanders approach to life? Next week you'll have them eating sushi on roller skates."

Zan grinned in spite of herself. "Whatever works."

Stu dropped the pencil he'd been fingering and it skittered across the desk. He leaned forward on his fists and pinned her with his gaze. Zan willed herself not to step back and she met his look with a surface calmness.

"Zan Flanders, you are driving me crazy. You are an infuriating, irritating, aggravating—"

"Don't forget fascinating."

"Pigheaded, pertinacious—"

"Can you spell that?"

"Nuisance!" Stu had gotten steadily closer as he'd rapped out each adjective, and now his face was only inches from hers. Beneath the annoyance Zan could see a familiar flicker in the azure eyes, and she allowed herself one deep sharp breath.

"Will you cancel the project?" Stu asked softly.

"No." She returned his glare.

Their gazes locked for several long moments in a silent battle. Without moving, Zan asked, "Now what? I mean," she explained, her eyes remaining on Stu's, "eventually there'll be certain bodily functions that have to be attended to. Like lunch."

A grin tugged at the edge of Stu's mouth, but before he could reply they heard three excited voices outside in the hall approaching her door.

"I most certainly remember volunteering for the second show before you, Faye, and you know it."

"I can't understand this dreary seniority system of yours, Amelia, and let's be absolutely fair, now. Who's the one who's been complaining on Saturday nights about the lack of eligible males and who's the one who's been content to be watching 'Love Boat'?"

"That's totally besides the point, Faye. Just because I'm not a sex maniac..."

"Well, I do advise you to try it some time, it's quite delightful, you know."

"Will you two please stop bickering, I need you to help me pick out my date." Bertie swept into the office, looking radiant, followed by a disgruntled looking Amelia and Faye. "Hello Zan, Stu! We didn't expect to see you here."

Stu straightened up. "I came by to talk to Zan."

"Oh, then you must have seen the show last night. Wasn't it a marvelous idea?"

"Didn't Bertie look beautiful?" Amelia asked.

"She always does."

"I'm dying to see the letters," Bertie told Zan, and crossed to the desk. "Come here girls, help me look. Oh my! Who is this, Cary Grant?"

Faye and Amelia followed and began to leaf through the pile. "Look at this one," Amelia exclaimed. "A retired astrophysicist. How fascinating."

"Oh yes, darling," Faye said. "I can just picture his dinner table conversation; he'll put you right to sleep in the mashed potatoes. Oh, now here's one for you, Bertie. He's in terrific shape. Look, he sent you a picture of himself in a bathing suit."

"How odd. What does he do?"

"With that chest, who cares? I just hope he'd do it with me."

"Faye!"

Zan looked over the heads of the women and followed Stu with her eyes as he walked over to the window and stood looking out, his back to the room. His posture looked proud and angry. He put one foot up on the radiator, causing the material of his jeans to fit even more snugly along his hips and thighs. An ache welled up in her throat and she looked away.

"Oh, I don't know who to choose. Zan, our first date is next Saturday night, right? Where are we going?"

Zan kept her eyes on Stu's broad back while she answered. "It's a new wave dance club called Club Fun."

"Sounds wonderful, I can't wait. You know, I've felt twenty years younger since you came up with this. I even skipped my laxative this morning."

"I hope I get this many letters," Amelia said, still pondering the astrophysicist.

"If you don't take Hugo Zigmond, I will." Faye sighed and put down the photograph. "Great legs."

"Zan what time should I be ready on Saturday? I'll probably need the whole week to prepare. You know, I read that egg whites on your face can really tighten up your skin. Maybe we should pick up a couple of dozen on the way home."

Faye shuddered. "Sounds dreadful, and don't be silly Bertie darling, you're gorgeous."

Zan looked over at Stu but there was still no response. "About six o'clock I think, Bertie, since we'll be doing the interviews first. What do you think, Stu?" She waited. If he refused she knew she'd find it hard to continue with the project.

Stu didn't turn and when he spoke his voice was flat and expressionless. "Sounds fine to me."

"So who is your date going to be, Zan?" Amelia asked.

"He's a stockbroker who moonlights as a new wave musician. Club Fun was his choice for his favorite date."

"What's his name? He sounds fascinating."

"Well, he is a little unorthodox."

"All the better," Faye said flatly. "What did you say his name was?"

"Neil S. Beauwinkle, III. But his friends call him Sludge."

Sludge bobbed up and down and played air guitar with great concentration while Stu went ahead of the long line outside Club Fun to tell the manager they'd arrived. Zan watched him thread easily through the crazily dressed crowd as Bertie and her date chattered behind her.

They had all been surprised when Bertie had chosen Gaspar Jourdan as her escort, whose tall dark good looks were distinctly exotic. Born in Guadeloupe, he had lived in the Bay Area for forty years and still owned a successful winery in Mendocino up the coast. Bertie had instantly been struck by his picture, in which he looked brooding and very French, and after she'd read his short letter she hadn't looked further. He'd simply stated that when he'd seen her on television he'd experienced a *coup de foudre*—a sudden, thunderstruck passion for her—"and that is saying something for a man of my age." Bertie had called him immediately, and they'd chatted on the phone every night over the past week. Faye had pointed out that Bertie was merely finally fulfilling her youthful fantasies about Charles Boyer, but Bertie had just gone on being dreamy eyed. And by the look of Gaspar Jourdan tonight, Zan decided, she wasn't the only one.

Sludge continued his assault on his imaginary guitar, but when she caught his eye he grinned at her. With the green washed out of his hair, he was actually not bad looking, with a kind of devil-may-care look in his eye that Zan was sure women would find appealing. He'd been articulate and oddly winning in the interview, claiming that his unorthodox life-style on weekends was his way of reconciling his creative side with his uncanny money-making abilities as a successful and very orthodox stockbroker.

Yet he had said that it was hard for him to develop a relationship with a woman. Maybe they got turned off by the sight of a thirty-two-year-old in orange zebra-patterned high-top sneakers, Zan mused. Or the addiction to air guitar. But she had a feeling it had more to do with the fact that his notion of an ideal first date was to take a woman to a crowded and deafeningly loud club and shout at her across a dance floor. Was it any wonder he found it hard to get to know them?

Zan perched on the edge of an equipment case and contemplated how many cans of styling mousse had gone onto the carefully tousled heads of the crowd in line. She'd had fun dressing up for this evening, but she felt strangely out of place. Gaspar and Bertie seemed more relaxed than she, and even Sludge, who was three years her senior, made her feel old. Maybe it was because having fun was usually work to her. If she went to an opening or to the theater, her mind was constantly clicking off ideas for a column about it. Tonight she was storing up images for her voice-over on the tape.

But there was something else, she admitted grudgingly, and it had to do with a large scruffy man who hadn't looked twice at her all evening. Zan hadn't realized how much she'd been dressing with Stu in mind until he'd arrived at her door and treated her like a prop. She'd gotten a gush of compliments from Bertie and a long lingering kiss on the hand from Gaspar, who had murmured that she was *"une femme extraordinaire,"* but Stu had only asked her to test the mike, and was there any coffee made?

The little black dress was loose at the neckline, occasionally slipping off one shoulder artfully, but tight at the sleeves and along the skirt, which ended slightly above her knee. She had drawn up her hair into a wonderfully flashy rhinestone clip, she had worn black lace stockings and high-heeled pumps, and she hadn't made a dent in those impassive features. Worst of all, she'd spent the entire night wondering why she wanted to. She ran her hands up and down her arms nervously, and Jack, Stu's assistant, leaned over.

"Here comes Stu, Zan. We'll be inside in a minute."

Zan stood up. She was tired of feeling sorry for herself, anyway. She extended one leg behind her, then the other, to check if the seams of her stockings were straight. When she turned forward again, she found Stu stopped a few feet away, watching her.

The harsh glare of the spotlights outside the club cast his features into bold relief and made him look dangerous. His eyes were glittering, blue as winter shadows, and his normally full mouth looked grim and hard. For a moment she stood motionless, frozen by his cryptic regard. The sound of the crowd, the murmurs of Bertie and Gaspar, the heavy insistent beat of music from the club, all melded into the softest whisper of sound, lapping at her consciousness, barely there. The harsh light went misty and centered around Stu. There was only Stu. Something inarticulate and important pounded in Zan's head and then found a voice. *This is it,* the voice said, insistent and steady. *This is it.* Her pulse pounded to that instinctual cry, and Stu moved forward. Then Bertie touched her arm, and the mood broke, shattered, letting in the sounds of the night and the raucous strains of music. The light became harsh and bright once more.

Zan took a short step back, shaken. She didn't know what had just happened, what it meant, and she couldn't face it. She shook her head.

"Zan?" Bertie's voice was concerned. "Are you all right?"

"Fine." She sternly forced herself to return to the world. She turned and smiled at Bertie. "I'm fine. Stu's back; let's go inside and dance."

She picked up a piece of equipment and followed Bertie and Gaspar, not daring to look at Stu again. She told herself that it had been a momentary spell of dizziness, and it served her right. She'd skipped dinner out of nervousness, and she'd paid the consequences.

But somewhere a small voice nagged at her insistently, asking if she would continue to blame her unsettled feelings about Stu on the vagaries of her digestive system.

Sludge took her free arm as they entered, and she handed the equipment case to Jack. "Now you'll see why I think this place is so dynamite," Sludge yelled over the music. "Great sound. Dance floor is surrounded by mirrors. You can really check out your moves. Come on, I'll show you the swimming pool."

Colored lights pulsated over Zan's head and a shimmering globe fractured light onto the walls, lending the built-in aquariums a surrealistic air. She peered into a tank, wondering what the disagreeable-looking fish was.

"Barracuda!" Sludge shouted into her ear. "Cool!"

She shivered, and followed Sludge down to another level, which was dominated by a large swimming pool. Floating gaily on top of the water was an assortment of childish water wings. Plastic palm trees in fluorescent oranges, pinks and greens towered over them, and waiters dodged among the crowd wearing Bermuda shorts and sports shirts in contrasting wild patterns, with black socks and sandals.

"It's called the Miami Beach Room," Sludge said.

"Does anyone ever swim in the pool?"

"Nah. Unless you get thrown in. Well, do you want to dance? Or we could go up to the third level. There's a performance artist—or is it a process artist?—showing a twenty-minute slow-motion video of himself touching his tongue to the tip of his nose while he plays one of his own compositions on a touchtone phone."

"I think I might have seen that one already," Zan said. "Oh, there's Bertie." She threaded her way through the crowd on the dance floor and shouted in Bertie's ear. "Where's Stu? What should we do?"

"Dance! Stu said to go ahead and have fun and he'll find us. He's shooting the rest of the place."

Sludge grabbed her arm and swung her around. He had an odd kind of grace as a dancer, and Zan found that she was actually enjoying herself as they moved around the floor. They danced several numbers, Zan finally getting the hang of Sludge's unique bobbing jitterbug style. When he whipped her around in a particularly fast twirl, she found herself losing her balance, and she whirled straight into Stu and his camera.

Stu's free arm shot out and steadied her with an iron grip. She leaned against him, breathless, for an instant.

"You're working especially hard this evening, Zandra," he said, his mouth close to her ear. "I do admire your dedication."

She pushed away from him abruptly and threaded back into the mass of slithering muscular bodies who were trying not to look at themselves on giant video screens. She felt no more at home in this place than Stu did; why did he make her feel like a dizzy social butterfly?

The music changed to a slow ballad, and Sludge swept her into his arms again. They circled around slowly while Stu made a wider circle around them, his lens trained on their faces.

Sludge frowned in Stu's direction. "He does take his work seriously, doesn't he?"

"Like death and taxes." Zan thought of the earlier interview with Sludge, when he'd spoken of his obsession with his music. His words about being lost up on stage, alone with the pulse of the music, almost exactly echoed Toby Jones's description of windsurfing on the bay. She felt sure that Stu's words about his camera would sketch the same kind of solitary obsession. It seemed that they all had a way to remove themselves from the world, and it was the focal point of their lives. It was the outstanding trait of the Bachelor of the 80's.

The music stopped and Bertie approached to whisper to Zan. "What's going on with Stu? He won't let you and Sludge alone. Is he jealous?"

The music began again and she yelled back at Bertie over the driving beat, "You've got to be kidding." Bertie had a chance to shrug before Sludge whirled her away.

Zan declined Gaston's offer of a dance and went over to perch on an unsteady makeshift couch fashioned from inflatable rafts tied together. She watched Stu, grinning widely, shoot Bertie and Sludge's dance, and her eyelids began to droop. She'd always believed she could fall asleep anywhere, and now she proceeded to prove it.

"You have to be exhausted." The voice close to her ear made her jump, and she turned to find Sludge at her side. "How could you possibly fall asleep in this place? I know, novices always tire early. Come on, I'll drive you home. I told Bertie to let Stu know we'd left."

Zan nodded wearily and let Sludge guide her to his car. She leaned back against the headrest and soon found herself slipping off to sleep again as Sludge headed for the Golden Gate Bridge. She didn't wake until he pulled up in front of her door.

"Come on, lovely lady, I'll walk you home." Sludge turned off the ignition and walked her up the flagstone path.

She yawned when they reached the front door. "Thank you, Sludge. I know it was out of your way to bring me home." She stuck out her hand. "Good night."

Sludge took her hand and held on to it a little too long. He stepped closer. "Don't I get a kiss good night?" Before she could protest, his mouth came down on hers.

Zan had forgotten how irritating an unwanted kiss could be. She gently pushed against his chest, and Sludge immediately withdrew. Suddenly a bright light shone in their faces and she heard a slow amused voice.

"That's all right, go right ahead with what you were doing," Stu said from behind his camera. He moved a step closer and trained the lens on them. "Don't mind me at all."

Chapter Six

Zan stepped out of the circle of Sludge's arms. Stu peered around the camera at her.

"Really, don't mind me. Go right ahead. Perfect ending to the date."

Sludge walked toward Stu slowly, and Zan tensed. But he merely said something to him that she couldn't catch, and she saw Stu look startled. Then Sludge turned back to her and saluted. "Guess it's time to call it a night. It's a night, Zan."

She nodded, smiling. "It's a night." He got into his car and took off with a final wave.

Stu sighed heavily. "Oh dear. I'm afraid I keep scaring off your admirers."

"And you seem really concerned about it." Zan stifled a laugh. "Actually, I have to admit I was more than a little relieved to see you. Saved me from the single man's 'Will I Get Lucky Litmus Test.' "

Stu grinned and eased the camera off his shoulder. "What's that?"

"Oh, you know, the good-night kiss that rates your responsiveness and the chances of the evening ending up in a more, uh, compromising position. Most men tend to overrate the response."

"Hope springs eternal," Stu said. He set the camera down and took a step toward her. "What's the matter, Zan?" he asked deliberately. "Do you have something against good-night kisses?"

She took a step back and ended up against the door. "Well, no, of course not. It just depends on the kisser and the kissee."

"I see." Stu took another step.

"I mean, there has to be a mutual, well, interest."

"Mmmm. Interest, you say. Sounds very matter-of-fact."

"Well, more than interest, I guess. Desire."

The moonlight glittered behind Stu as he put each hand against the door behind her head. "Desire. Much better than 'mutual interest,' wouldn't you say?"

"I suppose." Zan paused as Stu reached out with one finger to trace the curve of her cheek, a touch that was feather-light and subtly arousing. "Stu?"

The finger moved on to her bottom lip. "Mmmm?"

She swallowed. "Would you like a peanut butter and jelly sandwich and a glass of milk?"

The finger paused. "Would I like a peanut butter and jelly sandwich?"

She nodded.

"And a glass of milk?"

She nodded again.

Stu took a deep breath and let it out slowly. "Sure."

Zan turned and fumbled her key into the lock. Perhaps peanut butter and jelly would be innocent and prosaic enough to defuse the charged atmosphere. She was confused by Stu's sudden advances, and she needed time to get her bearings. She was uneasy at the thought of letting him into her house in the early morning hours, but she couldn't bear to let him go.

She pushed open the door finally and led the way downstairs to the dining room. Motioning to a chair, she ordered, "Sit down and I'll get the sandwich fixings."

"Let me help you."

Zan put a hand on Stu's chest and gently pushed him into a chair. "Oh no, you're not," she said softly. "Do you think I'm crazy enough to get in a kitchen with you again?"

Stu gave her a knowing look and grinned wickedly. "Hope springs eternal." He looked down at her hand, which had remained on his chest of its own accord.

Zan snatched it away. "I'll get the food." A low chuckle followed her into the kitchen, and she prepared a tray wondering at her own foolishness. Did she think this was going to be easy? When she returned to the dining room she placed the tray on the table firmly and said, "Let's talk about work."

"All right," Stu said mildly. He spread some peanut butter on the whole-grain bread and reached for the strawberry jam. "How come you're not married?"

"What does that have to do with work?"

"Nothing." Stu took a bite of his sandwich.

"Why do you want to know?"

"I don't know. Maybe it's because you're such a culinary whiz, and your talents are going so sadly unnoticed. You whipped this meal up in seconds. I'm very impressed."

"I try not to call too much attention to it. Why aren't *you* married?"

"I asked you first. Have you ever come close?"

"I was engaged once."

The sandwich stopped halfway to Stu's mouth. "What happened?"

Zan sighed. "Todd was a fairly typical underweight lawyer who decided it was time he 'got into fitness.' He joined a health club downtown and started spending all of his free time there working out."

"So you broke up with him?"

Zan nodded. "What else could I do? He started beating me at tennis."

Stu laughed softly. "What really happened, Zan?"

She creased the napkin in her lap. "One evening I went down to the club to pick him up; it was a surprise. It was late, and I poked around, looking in all the empty exercise rooms. He'd been taking individual aerobics classes, said that his instructor had recommended it. So finally I pushed open one door and the first thing I saw was a pair of crumpled pink spandex tights in the middle of the floor. Then I saw Debbi, Todd's aerobics instructor. She and Todd were reflected about a million times in all those mirrors." Zan gave a short laugh. "For a second I didn't know if he was cheating on me or developing a new aerobics routine."

Stu didn't laugh. "That's really lousy," he said quietly.

"It was for the best, actually." Strange how easily the words came out when it had taken her so long to believe they were true. It had only been in the past year that she'd fully realized that she'd never been in love with Todd at all. He'd merely said the right things and made the right offer at a very turbulent time.

Zan poured Stu another glass of milk. "So now you have to answer the same question."

He shrugged. "Never even came close. My brothers make up for me, anyway. They both have such happy marriages it's almost obnoxious to get together with them and my parents."

"Where do they live?" Zan asked, laughing at Stu's grimace.

He shifted in his chair and reached over to toy with the tendrils on the back of her neck. "Boston. One brother is a painter, as well as as my mother. My other brother is an oboe player and my father is an art dealer."

"Quite a family. Everyone's an artist of some kind."

"Except for me."

"What do you mean? You're a filmmaker."

Stu was busy following the draped neckline of her dress with his finger. "A *documentary* filmmaker. And thus, a black sheep. My family lives in a world of art and music, and I barge in talking about politics and revolutions. I dropped out of art school to study filmmaking at New York University. I thought that art should *do* something, change things."

"And what do you think now?"

"I still think so." Stu sighed. "But it gets harder. It's funny, the older I get, the *less* callous I get, the more involved I get with my subjects. I don't know how good that is for my films. I'm starting to question my objectivity."

"That doesn't sound so tragic. It sounds human."

"It's tragic for a documentarian."

"I don't know about that. But my general rule is, when you find yourself in a new direction, keep following your nose."

Stu felt his nose and grinned. "In my case, that wouldn't be terribly difficult."

Zan grinned back. The usual thunderous heat she felt around Stu had been replaced by a surprisingly quiet tenderness, and when Stu brought her fingers to his lips and kissed them gently she drew comfort from the friendliness of the gesture.

Then she looked up at him again and the tenderness shifted inside her, carrying with it now the beginning flickers of arousal. She could see the same change of mood in Stu's eyes, she could feel the sudden tenseness in the air, and a small sound of surprise escaped her.

The clock in the kitchen ticked away several long seconds. It was close to three o'clock in the morning, and the world had suddenly dropped away outside the dark panes of her windows. She was lost inside a moment that would surely go on forever, waiting for Stu to make a sign.

He looked away and glanced at his watch. "It's late."

"Yes."

"I should go."

"Yes."

He stood. "Well..."

Zan trailed behind him up the stairs, her eyes level with a very appealing part of his anatomy. She clumped up the stairs disconsolately. Confusion still reigned in her where Stu Temple was concerned, but one thing was certain: the man had a great rear view.

She sank down on the couch in the living room as Stu put on his jacket. He perched on the edge and looked at her.

"Tired?"

"Mmmm. Peanut butter and jelly at three o'clock in the morning always knocks me out." Zan suddenly remembered a question she'd meant to ask him earlier. "Stu, what did Sludge say to you before he left tonight?"

"Nothing, really."

"Oh come on, tell me."

For the first time since she'd met him, Stu looked embarrassed. "He apologized."

"Apologized? Why? You were the one who nearly blinded him with a klieg light."

Stu studied the material of the couch intently. "He said he hadn't realized that we were, uh, involved."

"That we were— Oh."

"He left before I could explain that we weren't."

"Oh."

"Because we're not."

"Right."

"Are we?"

"Are we what?"

"Involved." Stu began to grin.

"No, of course we're not. Well, what do you mean, exactly?"

Stu slid off the arm of the couch and bumped down next to her. "Well, for instance, what happens when we do this?" Suddenly she was in his arms. The kiss was velvet and satin, insinuating, soft. His mouth was supple and slightly sticky from strawberry jam, and she sighed against its sweetness. She felt the rough tweed of his jacket underneath her fingers and the line of one hard thigh along her leg.

Stu pulled just a hair's breadth away. "You see, we're involved when we kiss," he murmured.

"We can't stay with our mouths locked together all the time," she whispered back.

"We can't?"

"Look, Stu, hormones may be raging, but we're not kids anymore. That can't be everything. We have to be sensible."

"That's a change of attitude."

"It is?"

He stood and reached out a hand to help her up. "I quote from a well-known San Francisco columnist: 'Sensible is a concept that should be reserved for shoes that one must resist buying under any circumstances. Never let it be used to describe you.' Sound familiar?"

"I'm afraid so. But I never claimed to be consistent."

"Then I bow to your eminently sensible attitude. Now, back to business. There's a Sausalito town council meeting this Thursday night. They're going to decide on the eviction at the Perdue Home. The ladies want you to be there."

Just the ladies, not Stu. "Of course I'll come."

"Should be tough. Faye has been designated the spokesperson for the Home by the members, and Dwayne Perdue won't even be there. He's content to remain behind the scenes. I've gotten permission to show a clip from my documentary. Sometimes seeing how things are instead of just hearing about them can help. Meeting starts at seven-thirty, we can go together if you want. Call me next week sometime. Good night, Zan."

Stu headed out the door into a night glittering with stars. He walked down the dark path without a backward glance, with not a word or a look of regret. Of course, she could take consolation from the fact that she'd been eminently sensible. She had been the one to hold fast to a businesslike relationship. Zan numbly watched Stu's taillights disappear down the street. She'd never felt so bereft at a man's ability to take a hint.

* * *

Stu's office was south of Market Street in San Francisco, an area that had been a rather rundown accumulation of wholesale businesses, warehouses, and industrial buildings, but was now host to film and video companies, artists, and designers. New restaurants, galleries, and clubs sprang up every week, it seemed. But best of all for Zan was that Stu's office was an easy ten-minute walk from the *Modern Times* offices.

She was running late; they had barely a half hour to get to the town council meeting, and they still had to fight commuter traffic to get across the bay to Sausalito. Zan raced up the stairs to the office, knocked once on the door, and pushed.

The door opened a few inches, then stopped. She leaned her weight against it, but it didn't budge. Zan peered through the crack. "Stu?" There was no answer. She called again, louder.

"Yo!" The answering call came from the back recesses of the office, and a few seconds later the sound of something heavy being moved came from behind the door. It swung open and Jack Frost appeared, nodding at her. "Hiya, Zan. Sorry about that. I've been tearing the place apart looking for the fish food. Stu's not here yet. Told me to tell you to wait for him, he's on his way. Oh, c'mon in."

"Thanks, Jack." By now Zan was used to the casual chaos of Stu's office and Jack's steady clipped barrage of information. She stepped inside. What never ceased to amaze her was that they ever located anything at all, but Stu always seemed to be able to pluck anything they needed from the debris instantly. "Isn't the fish food on top of the filing cabinet?"

"Should be but it isn't." Jack ran his hand through his red hair. "And Mooch is looking mighty hungry."

"What I still don't understand is," Zan said, looking under a pile of papers for the container, "how an innocent goldfish could possibly be a mooch."

"Stu says it's the way Mooch watches him while he eats lunch."

Zan gingerly picked up a stale half-eaten sandwich with a mysterious grayish filling and dropped it in the garbage can. "The poor fish is probably just nauseated."

Jack chuckled as he stacked tapes on the editing console. "Might as well organize this stuff while I'm looking. So you're going to the town council meeting tonight?"

"If Stu ever gets here. Why don't you let me help you with that?"

"Oh, thanks. Could you just label a few of these tapes for me? We've started to transfer Stu's film to tape to show to community groups later on. Copy the title from the master list here—blue marker for Stu's documentary, red marker for yours—and then stick it on the tape. Like this. I hear the meeting could be rough for the ladies."

Zan picked up a felt-tip marker to label the tapes. "How so? Do things really look bad?"

"We've been hearing rumors about the women in the Home not being able to take care of themselves."

"That's ridiculous."

"Yup. Rumors are, sometimes. But people still believe them. Dwayne Perdue is probably behind it, I'm sure, but he doesn't want to seem like the bad guy so he's keeping under cover. We haven't been able to find him for an interview for the film. Anyway, the drift is that if the women were evicted they could be put into 'proper' homes and get medical care."

Zan frowned as she stuck a label on a tape. "Well, at least a clip from the documentary will help. People will see the women as they really are."

Jack shook his head. "Stu's the best documentarian I know," he said, straightening a stack of files absently. "You can't find a better, in my opinion. But you might say he lacks the personal touch. He's not much of a politician. He's heard the rumors too, and he's picked a clip to show tonight that he thinks is his strongest scene so far. But it's the reminiscences of Olivia Grandee, the oldest member of the Home. It *is* a strong scene—very touching, very powerful and all—but Livie comes off as a bit weak and sickly. Stu filmed her on a gray afternoon when she was just getting over the flu. Who wouldn't come off as weak? Not to mention that, well, Livie's not exactly the sharpest thing around even on her good days. Anyway, dramatically, the scene works, but it might just reinforce all those rumors about the ladies."

Zan stopped writing and looked up. "Did you tell Stu what you thought?"

"Sure. Stu listens, but he's, well, a little strong-minded. Likes to do things his way. I guess you haven't realized that about him yet."

Zan bent her head again to hide her smile. "I've had hints."

"It's one of the reasons he always produces his own films. He likes to have sole control, make his own decisions. I have to admit he's usually right."

Was "usually" good enough odds for the meeting tonight? Zan wondered. She looked down at the list she was copying without really seeing it. It was typical of Stu to try and bulldoze his way through the meeting, not taking into account the receptiveness of his audience. He would arrogantly rely on their good sense and fairness to make the right decision. Zan supposed it was an admirable quality of his, but she took a more jaundiced view of things. If the people were being manipulated by rumors, shouldn't they try to counter them in the most effective way they could?

The letters of the words she had just written on labels swam before her eyes. *Livie's Reminiscences*, read one; *Bertie at Club Fun*, said the other. She remembered both tapes vividly. Jack was right. If she didn't know Livie, she'd think she was infirm, and possibly slightly dotty. Coupled with the rumors, people might think she should be taken care of in a nursing home, instead of living in a self-care facility.

But Bertie had bounced joyfully on the dance floor with Sludge, good-naturedly trying to copy his slick moves. They'd added a voice-over from the interview, where Bertie had talked of the need for vitality and an interest in the world around one as one grew older.

Wasn't Bertie the more accurate picture of the true spirit of the Paradise Perdue Home?

"Hi, Jack. Sorry I'm late." Stu strode through the door with a black expression. "I was dealing with the boneheads at the film lab. They 'misplaced' some film. Can you believe it? Hi, Zan."

"Hello. Stu, listen, before we go, I—"

"Right, I'll be ready in a minute, Zan. Any messages, Jack?"

"Yes, here. But Mooch is starving. Where's the fish food?"

Stu leafed through the slips of paper Jack had handed him. "I filed it. Time we got organized around here."

"What did you file it under?"

"Oh. Good question. Try M."

"Not here."

Zan cleared her throat. "Stu—"

"Hmmm, how about F? Of course! For 'fish.'"

"Or food," Zan pointed out.

"Good thinking, Zan. If you ever need a job, let me know, okay?"

Jack sprinkled fish food on top of the water. "Sorry I can't introduce the clip tonight, Stu."

"That's okay."

"I mean, Janine's folks will only be in town one night, and this is it."

"It's *okay*, Jack. No problem. I can do it."

Zan looked over at Stu. "Are you nervous about speaking in front of a crowd?"

"No, of course not."

"Oh. Because lots of people do get nervous. All those eyes, staring at you..."

"I-am-not-nervous," Stu said tightly.

"It's nothing to be embarrassed about."

"Zan. Let's just drop the subject, okay?"

"Sure. But I do know this great relaxation exercise." Zan stopped at the murderous look in Stu's eye. "Just in case," she added lamely. "Funny that you, of all people, should be bothered by—"

"Jack, I'll see you tomorrow morning. Oh, Livie's tape. Where is it?"

"Stu, before we go, I wanted to—"

"Zan, we're late."

"I realize that. I, too, can read a watch. But I wanted to talk to you for a minute about the strategy for tonight."

"You want to talk about strategy?"

"Yes. I think we should discuss what clip to show tonight."

"You and me?"

She nodded. "Incredible as it may seem, I have an opinion."

"And I'm sure it's a very interesting one, but I've already picked the tape."

"But I think—"

Stu looked at his watch. "Zan, I've been in the documentary business for fourteen years. How long has it been for you, a month now? I don't know why you feel you have to persist in telling me how to run my business. Believe it or not, I was doing fine before you came along. Just fine, okay? Perfect, in fact."

"Obviously. I've heard your name proclaimed around the world as the savior of the poor and downtrodden. You're right up there with Gandhi. So why take advice? I bet Edward R. Murrow never did."

"If we stand here arguing, we'll be late for the meeting."

"If we hadn't argued, we could have had our discussion already."

"Well, now it's too late. Let's go." Stu spun on his heel and started toward the door. "Bring the tape, will you?" he called over his shoulder.

Zan wondered if a videotape thrown with enough force could inflict damage on a six-foot-three man with a petrified brain. Maybe it would at least knock some sense into him.

Or maybe there was another way a tape could knock sense into Stu Temple. Zan walked slowly back to the editing table where she'd been labeling the tapes. She watched as, almost of their own volition, her hands stuck the label *Livie's Reminiscences* on the tape of Bertie at

Club Fun. She turned around, her heart pounding, to see Stu waiting for her at the door.

He scowled. "Ready? You have the tape?"

She crossed to the door and handed it to him. "Okay, let's go."

Stu gave the tape a pat before putting it under his arm. "Wait until they get a load of this at the meeting."

Oh no, Stu, Zan told him silently as she followed him out the door, her palms damp in agonized anticipation. *Wait until you get a load of it now...*

Chapter Seven

Faye was waiting for them on the steps of the Sausalito city hall, huddled in a voluminous red cape that almost exactly matched the tip of her nose, which she was wiping with a wrinkled tissue. She blew her nose vigorously and peered out at them, looking haggard for the first time since Zan had met her.

"Good evening," she said, sniffing. "I must warn you, I have a terrible cold. I caught it from Livie, who's now fit as a fiddle, the rat. Amelia's in bed with it, and Bertie's out with Gaston. She's too happy to get sick. They're stopping by after dinner to hear the verdict."

"Faye, I know this is important, but shouldn't you be home in bed?" Zan asked worriedly.

"I don't believe in coddling myself, Zan," Faye answered, and sneezed with a trumpetlike flourish. Stu handed her his handkerchief. "Thank you, dear, I'll have to launder this before I return it. Where was I? Oh yes, I did take a couple of cold pills."

"A couple?" Zan whispered as they entered the council meeting room. They filed into a row in the back.

"Amelia gave them to me with instructions to take one every eight hours, but she's such a cautious thing, poor darling, so I took two. Don't worry, I have the constitution of an elephant. I'll be fine by the time I have to speak. I have *such* a lovely speech, you can't imagine."

"I can't wait." Zan looked around the room and noticed for the first time that it appeared the meeting would be packed to the rafters. It looked as though the entire population of Sausalito was there.

She looked over at Stu. By the time they had reached Sausalito, they had been almost cordial again. Stu had made an effort on the way over to be friendly, and she'd had the feeling he had regretted his dismissal of her at his office. But he hadn't regretted it enough to ask what she'd wanted to talk to him about, she'd noted, so although she was decidedly nervous about her switching of the tapes, she still felt justified. Sort of. Tapping Stu on the shoulder, she whispered, "Why do you think there's so many people here tonight?"

He frowned. "I don't think it's because of the Perdue Home. I think it's because of Howie the Clam. Can't hurt us, though."

Zan wondered if she was catching Faye's cold; she couldn't have heard Stu correctly. "Howie the what?"

The sharp rap of the gavel interrupted her. "This meeting will come to order," a tall businesslike woman said authoritatively. Zan admired the sleek lines of her tailored gray suit.

"That's Janet Tibbles, the head of city council," Stu whispered.

"I like her suit," Zan whispered back. Stu shot her a disgusted look, and she supposed it had been the wrong thing to say. She should be concentrating on more important issues, she supposed. She snuck a look at the tape in Stu's lap. Would her switching the tapes prove her to be a sober, serious sort to Stu? Somehow she doubted it.

Janet Tibbles rattled some papers and the buzzing that had been going on stopped abruptly. It seemed as though the whole room leaned forward in anticipation. "Now, for the main order of business," she announced. "Voting on the approval of the license for the fast-food chain of Howie the Clam, for the operation of a restaurant on the waterfront in town." There was a scattering of boos, and she looked at the crowd grimly over her half-glasses. "I refuse to tolerate any nonsense this evening. We will deal with Howie the Clam fairly, and I want you all to know that any decision will be supported with relish."

"No cocktail sauce?" Zan asked under her breath. Stu was ignoring her, and she nudged Faye to get her attention. When she got no response, she looked over and discovered that she was fast asleep.

"Wake up, Faye!" she hissed, but Faye's breathing was deep and regular, and she didn't budge. She shook her briskly, and Faye opened one eye.

"Just taking a little nap, darling, don't worry," she said. "I have a constitution like an elephant." Then she fell back asleep.

"Faye, please wake up," Zan pleaded in a frantic whisper, but she only settled deeper into her chair with a satisfied sigh. Zan nudged Stu and pointed to Faye.

"For crying out loud, keep her awake," Stu said through clenched teeth.

"How?"

"I don't know. Talk to her, will you? Tell her about Janet Tibbles's suit."

But Faye looked so peaceful that Zan hated to wake her again. Maybe a catnap would do her good, and then she could wake her up when the Howie the Clam discussion wound down.

Apparently the tide was running against the crustacean, and there was little chance that he would ever get to beach himself on the main street of Sausalito. Everyone seemed to feel that behind the fast-food franchise loomed giant billboards and neon, and they argued their points vociferously. Zan enjoyed the crash course in the governing of her town, and was proud of the fierce love of Sausalito that prompted such theatrics. She felt herself begin to relax a bit about her switching of the tapes; surely this colorful, exuberant crowd would respond to Bertie dancing with Sludge to "Limited Nuclear Love."

After an indignant artist crushed a clam shell underneath his heel and vowed to build a political-action sculpture out of shells to barricade the town against fast-food clam rolls, Zan leaned over to whisper at Stu. "Isn't this wonderful?"

Stu only glowered. "This isn't politics, it's theater."

"I know. Isn't it wonderful?"

Stu's frown intensified, and Zan punched him amiably. "Oh, come on, Stu, lighten up. Or are you a secret Howie the Clam fan?"

Stu opened his mouth for what promised to be a furious reply, but Janet Tibbles banged the gavel. "I hate clams," he managed to get out of the corner of his mouth before she began to speak again.

"The vote shows the council to be unanimously opposed to the Howie the Clam franchise obtaining a license for the town of Sausalito, and in favor of the polite suggestion they look for space at Fisherman's Wharf across the bay." A burst of cheers and applause drowned her out, and she allowed herself a brief grin before continuing. "Now for the next order of business: the matter of the closing down of the Paradise Perdue Home for Retired Actresses, due to numerous infractions."

While Janet Tibbles outlined the different aspects of the deterioration of the Home, Stu drummed his fingers on his knees nervously.

"You'll be fine," Zan told him softly. "You don't have to say much."

"Don't worry about me. Concentrate on Faye. She's practically in a coma."

Zan frantically tried to poke Faye back to life. She only gave a surprised snort and looked up at Zan with heavy eyelids.

"Just tell me when I have to speak," she slurred.

"You have to speak. Now, Faye. Faye!"

"And now we'll hear from one of the members of the Perdue Home," Janet Tibbles announced. "She's agreed to speak on some of the problems they've encountered. Faye Foxe, if you're ready to stand, please?"

At the sound of her name, Faye sat up expectantly for one short moment before falling back into a cheerful sleep. Heads turned and Faye obliged the attention by giving a soft peaceful snore.

The heads swiveled back to the front. At least they only looked puzzled, Zan consoled herself, not annoyed. But Faye's ill-timed nap would only reinforce the prejudices about the women being infirm.

Janet Tibbles recovered quickly and went on to introduce Stu's clip. Stu shifted in his chair.

"Stu," Zan whispered, "don't worry about all the faces, once you get up there. Just look at me when you speak, okay?"

He had time for a quick nod before standing to make his way to the video monitor in the front of the room. Zan crossed her fingers as he loaded the tape. Maybe, just maybe, Bertie could save the day.

Stu stood in front of the room uneasily for a moment, his big hands hanging loosely at his sides. He scanned the crowd and found Zan. She smiled at him warmly, and one corner of his mouth lifted; it was a short smile, a private smile, and it was meant only for her.

"What you're about to see is an interview with a member of the Paradise Perdue Home," he said, his clear deep voice carrying across the room. "I think it will give you an idea of why the Home is so unique, as well as the hurdles these women face to remain together, and the spirit that keeps them going."

He pressed the play button and moved over to a side aisle. The heavy, hypnotic beat of "Limited Nuclear Love" began to pound, and Zan just had time to see Stu's startled expression before someone turned off the lights.

She knew every cut on the tape, every move Bertie made, every word she spoke, and Zan now concentrated on the audience reaction. After a short baffled pause, she heard the delighted laughter of people encountering the unexpected; instead of the depressing tale of woe they'd been primed for, they were being charmed by an exuberant woman with fuzzy gray hair who was bobbing about with a cheerful young fellow in orange sneakers.

Now that her eyes had adjusted to the darkness, Zan could make out Stu's tense form in the side aisle. It had been obvious that he'd been unpleasantly shocked by the tape that had appeared, but he'd made no move to turn it off. Zan clasped her hands together and discovered that her fingers were still crossed. She untwined them carefully. She didn't need luck to handle Stu when he returned to his seat. Common sense would win the day. Even Stu couldn't argue with the appreciative roars of the audience. How could they possibly turn the delightful Bertie out of her home?

Bertie did a last twirl for the camera, the skirt of her silver dress flaring out to reveal a pair of still lovely legs, and she made her last remark straight into the lens, the globe behind her shooting off glints of fractured colored light. Her expression turned serious. "Oh, if only life were this gay," she said.

The screen went dark, there was a pause, and then a burst of furious applause. Stu turned, plainly astonished at the feverish reaction. He slipped the tape out of the deck and quickly made his way back to his seat.

He sat down, shaking his head. "I don't understand it," he said in a low rapid tone. "Jack is usually so careful. We kept the tapes of my documentary and yours strictly separate. We coded and labeled them differently. Where did you get this tape?"

"Stu, I—"

The gavel rapped and they fell silent. They both waited, barely breathing, as the council voted to postpone their decision pending further evidence. Stu turned to her with a happy grin when the gavel banged for the last time.

"Not bad," he said. "Not bad at all. It gives us some time, at any rate."

"Maybe the tape mix-up actually helped us," Zan tried.

His smile instantly turned into a frown. "Now how—"

Zan took a deep breath. "Stu, I did it. I switched the tapes."

"What?"

"I switched them."

"I don't understand. Did you make a mistake, or what?"

"It wasn't a mistake. I did it deliberately. There were those rumors about the women's poor health, and I thought it would help our case if we showed a clip from my documentary instead of yours. We shouldn't reinforce their prejudices with a misleading tape. We can change their minds and entertain them at the same time. I think it worked, don't you?"

The knuckles of Stu's hand were white as he gripped the tape. "You go into my office and switch tapes without telling me just because you want everyone to have a good *time*? You throw out a tape that is an enlightening view of their struggles—"

"My tape was enlightening too!"

"Do you really think so? Do you really think that tape gave a good picture of what Bertie's life is like? Or the rest of the women? Do you think before you came along with your so-called 'documentary' that those women cavorted in nightclubs every Saturday night?"

"Of course not. But the tape shows that it *was* an unusual evening, and—"

"I don't understand you," Stu burst out suddenly in frustration. "And I don't understand why the fates have compelled me to be saddled with you. I'm a serious documentarian, and you're turning me into Groucho Marx!"

"We should only be so lucky."

"What?"

"Maybe that's the cure for you, Stu Temple. You should be sentenced to a weekend of nonstop Marx Brothers movies, one after the other. Maybe after seeing *Duck Soup* a few times you'll develop a sense of humor."

"I have a sense of humor."

"You do not."

Stu narrowed his eyes at her. "At least I don't have a coffee stain on my blouse." When Zan looked down, he placed his finger under her nose and lifted her head back up. "Gotcha."

"Very funny. If that's the level of your so-called humor, it's no wonder you stick to dreary documentaries. You got a *reaction* out of the audience tonight. Wasn't that a bit of a novelty for you, Stu?"

"I'll tell you what was a novelty," Stu said, his voice low with fury. "Having my work introduced and then discovering that a silly little piece for a video magazine was being passed off as my film. That's a novelty for you."

"That piece was your work too."

Stu shook his head. "No it wasn't. It's something I shot, not something I made. I would never put my name on that piece of—"

Zan stood up. "How dare you! Well, you don't have to *lower* yourself to the indignities of TV journalism anymore."

Stu stood up too, and glared down at her. Zan tilted her neck back to meet his eyes, wishing he had stayed put. It was easier to fire someone while looking down on him.

"Are you trying to fire me?" Stu asked with admirable calm. "First of all, you can't, only Mark McFee can. And second of all, I quit."

"Good."

"I just hope you haven't spoiled everything for the Perdue Home." Stu shook his finger at her. "And you'd better hope so too."

Fury galvanized Zan into action. She looked down at the finger pointing at her chest and bit it. "Don't threaten me, Stu Temple," she said evenly. "I get mean."

Just then Faye stirred behind her. "What a delightful nap," she said, yawning, then looked around at the empty room, surprised. "Where did everyone go? Don't I have to make my speech?"

"It's all over. They postponed the decision."

"Oh, lovely." She peered up at them. "And you two are having a nice chat, I can tell. Where are Bertie and Gaston? Heaven only knows what they've been doing all evening. On second thought, I know exactly what they've been doing, the lucky dogs."

Zan helped Faye up, smiling. "Come on, Faye, I'll help you find them. You should get to bed."

"That's just my point, Zan, I—Oh, isn't Stu coming with us?"

"No. There's a Marx Brothers triple feature on the late show that he doesn't want to miss." She tucked Faye's arm in hers and turned to the coldly furious Stu. "Give my regards to Groucho," she said, and swept up the aisle.

Zan dropped her socket wrench and bit back a howl of frustration. She might as well have coated her fingers with butter for all her failed attempts to hang on to various tools and stray spark plugs today. It would be a miracle if she managed to make it through Saturday with all her fingers and toes intact.

She'd decided this morning to give her '66 Mustang convertible a badly needed tune-up, but she was having a hard time concentrating on the task at hand. For the past two days she'd been grumpier than usual with Mark, snapped several dozen pencils in half and tried to do the same to a favorite fountain pen, and had even threatened to impale a rude cab driver with the sharp end of her umbrella. No, she hadn't exactly been at her best.

The problem was, she admitted grudgingly, that her conscience was bothering her, just a bit. Of course, she'd been absolutely justified in switching those tapes. She'd had the best interests of the ladies at heart, and Stu really had provoked her into it. Why, then, was a small voice tickling her brain, telling her that with any other person, she would never have done it? She'd have been tempted, but like the rational adult that she used to be before meeting Stu Temple, she would have refrained.

But the person involved was Stu, and that made all the difference. Brain cells had a tendency to dissolve when he was around. Zan savagely untwirled a spark plug and groaned. She knew very well that she was like a nettlesome wasp around Stu, intent on dive-bombing his head despite the swats that tried to keep her at bay. Wasn't there a small, mean-spirited part of her that got pleasure out of unsettling him?

She'd wakened staring that supposition in the face this morning, and the sheer horror of it had propelled her into faded jeans and a snug white T-shirt, her uniform for hard work, and straight into the garage with only a banana for breakfast. Changing spark plugs required no agonizing. It was the mature and sensible thing to do on a cloudy Saturday, and it would take her mind off the fact that lately maturity had been a rare commodity in her life. She was slowly regressing past adolescence straight back into childhood; hadn't she bit the end of Stu's finger Wednesday night? It had been just a nip, true, but at this rate she'd soon be sinking to the floor and bursting into tears like a three-year-old.

At least she didn't have to work with him anymore. He'd quit, and that was that. Zan wondered why she hadn't told Mark the news. Stu hadn't called him yet either, but she supposed they'd have to start looking for a new producer on Monday. Maybe Stu could recommend someone. Maybe she should call him and . . .

Zan squirmed deeper into the engine to bear down on an especially stubborn spark plug. Her brother Brody had always said that there was nothing like the smell of a motor to clear out the dust from your head. She sniffed experimentally and discovered that along with the oil and grime was a scent much more elusive and delicate. It smelled like . . . flowers?

"Hello, Zan." Stu's voice echoed across the cool garage.

Startled, she raised her head from the engine quickly and cracked it smartly against the raised hood. Swallowing an oath, Zan uncoiled herself from the engine and straightened.

Stu was standing at the entrance to her garage. He looked sleek and handsome in a white cotton shirt and casual olive green corduroys, his black hair neatly brushed off his forehead. He even looked as though he'd shaved that very morning.

"Hi," she finally managed. She noticed that he was carrying a lovely old-fashioned straw basket, tied with a purple ribbon, and full of white lilacs. He was probably on his way to bring it to the Perdue Home, Zan guessed.

She was speechless when Stu silently held out the basket to her. Wiping her hands on a handkerchief plucked from her rear pocket, she approached him slowly and took it from his hands. She buried her nose in the flowers; dewy and fresh, their scent gently chased away the gritty reality of the garage and the gloom of her morning. She looked up at Stu.

"They're lovely," she said awkwardly, "but why?"

Stu shrugged. "I was just passing by a florist on the way here and thought they looked pretty. Thought it might make it easier for you to apologize if I was nice first."

"For *me* to—" Zan choked back a sharp retort. She touched the lilacs tentatively with a slightly grubby finger. "I'm sorry I switched the tapes without telling you," she said into the flowers.

"You're forgiven." There was a short pause, and when Zan finally looked up, she saw Stu smiling faintly at her. "You'll notice," he said, "how gracious I can be. I'm not making you grovel."

"Don't push your luck, Stu. We were almost friendly there for a moment."

"'Almost friendly' is quite an achievement for us, isn't it? Look Zan, I know you were only trying to help the women. I really jumped down your throat."

"I guess I wasn't very nice either."

"We seem to have that effect on each other. I have a feeling that when we're not around each other, we can be pretty nice people."

"I've heard rumors to that effect."

"And we both have the same goal: to save the Perdue Home. I figure that if we're going to work together, we should try and be friends."

"Does that mean you're not quitting?"

"I like to complete my projects. And this one is very important to me." Stu smiled, holding her glance until Zan felt the need to examine her wadded up handkerchief. "Friends?" Stu asked, holding out his hand.

"Friends." She shook it, remembering her early resolution to avoid the custom with him. It had been a wise idea at the time; just the feel of his hard palm was enough to send her pulse rate soaring.

When Stu withdrew his hand it was splotched with grime. Laughing, Zan handed him her handkerchief. "That was not deliberate, I promise you."

Stu grinned and ambled farther into the garage. "So you're actually doing things to the engine of this heap?"

"Hey, I'll have you know that this car is a classic. What kind of a Californian are you, anyway?"

"I'm from Boston, remember? All I know is that this thing never runs." He ran his hand along the yellow paint. "At least it's the right color for a lemon."

Zan picked up her wrench. "I would think that a person who drives a station wagon that appears as though it spends its Saturdays at the demolition derby would watch what he says." She bent over the engine to remove a spark plug.

Stu handed her a new plug. "How long have you had it?"

"Seven years. My brother bequeathed it to me. He got it for his eighteenth birthday, and it was his baby. I've done my best, but I'm not the mechanic type, despite present appearances."

"Well, at least you're grimy enough to look official. Why doesn't your brother take it off your hands?"

Zan kept her eyes on the plug she was continuing to tighten, though it didn't need it. "He's dead."

She heard a sharp inhalation of breath behind her. "I'm sorry," Stu said quietly.

"It's all right. It happened a long time ago."

"How did it happen?"

She sighed into the engine; when would it get easier for her to talk about? "Brody was a photographer. He talked me into moving out here after I graduated from college, and then soon after I'd arrived he got this opportunity to go up to Alaska. A friend of his knew a pilot who flew mail all across the back country to various people who lived up there, miles from civilization. Brody thought it would make a great photographic essay—a dream assignment. I was uneasy; the weather had been bad, and the flying was done through dangerous conditions very often, but Brody had always gone anywhere, anytime, to shoot photographs. So he told me to take care of his house and his car and he went. Two weeks later the small plane he was traveling in was reported missing in the wilderness. It was another week before they found the wreckage. Then another two weeks before they found the bodies."

Her hands were idle now, but she remained bent over the engine, not willing to turn and face Stu. She continued, still staring at the wrench in her hands, "My brother and the pilot had apparently starting hiking away from the plane. They'd had a good sense of direction; another couple of days and they might have made it to a small settlement. But the storm that had driven them down was very bad, and they didn't make it. They died of exposure."

"That must have been awful for you."

Zan gave the plug a last futile twist and straightened. "Yes, it was," she answered shortly. Simple words for three weeks of agony, of assuring herself that of all the people in the world, Brody would survive. Hadn't he told her she could always depend on that? Hadn't he walked through an Asian jungle with a fractured ankle imagining Zan's taunt in their childhood game of "dare you"? *"Dare you to walk just one more mile, Brody."* He'd told her he had imagined her saying it on that frightening, feverish walk. And she had whispered, nights spent lying rigid, awake in her bed, *"Dare you to live, Brody. Dare you to make it out alive..."* When she'd finally received the terrible phone call, Todd had been forced to pry the receiver out of her white-knuckled grasp.

Now, seven years later, she looked down and discovered that she was grasping the wrench just as tightly as she had that receiver so long ago. Stu was looking down at her hand as well, and he quickly looked away as she carefully unclenched her fingers and wiped the wrench off with a rag. She spent a little time putting the rest of her tools away, grateful for the chance to put her memories away as well, grateful for Stu's silence and his pretended absorption in the car. She suddenly remembered how, during the long weeks after the news of Brody's death, Todd had never let her grieve; he would fill up any silences with chatter and diversions. She had thought she had needed that then; she had been terrified of confronting the silence. She had gone to Todd in relief, grateful for what she'd thought of as his strength, and just as gratefully promised to marry him. Now she wondered if Todd's technique had been good for her. He had been somehow threatened by her grief, afraid of it, and he had forced her to bury it quickly, with no time to mourn.

Zan snuck a look at Stu under her eyelashes and found him looking at her with serious eyes. He turned to look in the engine again, and she felt a strange warmth flood through her body. Here was a man who respected her privacy enough to be silent, but kept a watchful eye on her just the same. Here was a man who would offer her comfort if she made one tiny sign. He wasn't embarrassed or awkward in the presence of her grief; he was simply giving her time to recover.

She joined him by the car. "So you see," she said lightly as they stared into the engine, "it's not just a car, it's a sacred trust. I have gotten pretty good at tune-ups, though. Maybe if you're nice to me I'll take a look at that heap outside."

"Oh, I'd love to be *really* nice to you," Stu answered, "but you won't let me." He looked over at her. "I told you before, I can be amazingly nice."

"That wasn't exactly what I had in mind."

"Oh? Just what exactly do you think I have in mind?"

"Well, I— What exactly *do* you have in mind?"

Stu picked up her hands and turned them over, inspecting them. "If you're a good girl and go wash your hands, I'll treat you to a Chocolate Graham Cracker ice-cream cone at Mamie's."

"Okay, pops." Zan grinned and turned away, but not before feeling a flash of disappointment at Stu's response. This was what she got for regressing; the man she was just getting around to admitting she desired was now thinking of her as a six-year-old.

Chapter Eight

Fine, Stu. I'll meet you at the restaurant at six-fifteen. Yes, that's really the name of it. I didn't pick it, Claude Craven did. Yes, that's really his name. Is there anything else? Oh, I thought you started to say some— No, no, I just...no, nothing more on this end. See you there. Bye."

Zan hung up the phone and briefly considered throwing it against the wall. The only thing that stopped her was the certain knowledge that, with the *Modern Times* record for efficiency, she'd be collecting her pension before it was replaced.

Stu Temple had turned out to be, quite simply, the most aggravating man she'd ever met. He had reached new heights over the past weeks, even for him. He had the complete, unmitigated gall to be friendly, reasonably open to suggestions, and almost polite. She should have been rejoicing, but Zan knew it was all a devious plot to drive her insane.

It was all because of the enormous success of their series, "Modern Times on Screen." The Bay Area was buzzing with talk about the fast-paced, witty new series that raised provocative questions about the nature of intimacy, not only among the young, but among an older generation as well. The city had taken Amelia, Bertie and Faye to their hearts, and Zan could have sworn she'd been stopped on the street by every single man in San Francisco between the ages of fourteen and ninety, asking if they could take her or their particular favorite of the three women on their favorite "date."

The series had been a success beyond their wildest dreams, but the sweet taste of it had been spoiled for Zan by the fact that Stu never said a word about it. They might as well be in the bottom of the ratings basement for all he cared. He just went on doing his work, shooting the pieces, editing them with Zan, and not saying a single thing about the praise they had garnered.

Zan swiveled her chair around so that she could prop her legs on the radiator and look outside at the view. As always, her eyes invariably came to rest on the tiny sliver of bay she could glimpse between two skyscrapers. It was a crisp clear October day, and the startling blue of the water was the exact color of Stu's eyes. They were equally brilliant and equally cool. And, just as she had to struggle to catch the flash of blue amid the concrete, so it was just as difficult to capture what was going on in the cerulean depths of his eyes.

He had to be proud of his work, he had to. The success of the show was due as much to Stu as anyone. He was the one who paced the editing and pointed out the best visuals; he was the one who could edit an interview into clever, witty repartee; he was the one to juxtapose shots that could turn an ordinary scene into telling insight.

The placid silence had extended into their personal relationship as well. He bought her ice cream and discussed the next shoot and offered her a ride home in the same friendly tone he used with Jack. She'd even begun to miss his caustic remarks about the frivolity of her work. And he was so careful not to touch her, not an innocent brush of the hand, a tired pat on the shoulder, nothing. She missed it. Dangerous as it was, she missed it.

He knew it too, damn him. She was positive she'd seen a gleam of mischief in his eyes, as though he sensed her disappointment at his retreat. Just the other night they'd been editing until two o'clock in the morning, the night still and dark around them, and they might as well have been on Market Street in downtown San Francisco at the five o'clock rush hour for all the intimacy between them. She'd been on fire with the nearness of him, and when he'd finally driven her home and walked her to her door she'd turned to him with a body singing with expectant longing. *Just one kiss,* she'd thought, *that's all I want. Just one...*

Stu had taken her hand and looked deeply into her eyes. Then before she could begin to be surprised at the unexpected touch, he shook it briskly and dropped it. His expression had been cool and amused. "Good night, Zan. Sleep well." She'd tossed and turned all night.

"Slime mold," she growled at the bay.

"Troubles with your producer again?"

Zan swiveled her chair back to see Mark leaning into her office. "How'd you guess?"

"Fabulous intuition. I'd love to hear about it, but hang on to your hat, because Dwayne Perdue is on the phone for you. Just happened to be passing your secretary and thought I'd give you the news. How'd you manage to get ahold of him, anyway?"

"I dangled some bait." Zan waved Mark into her office and picked up the phone. "Zan Flanders."

"Ms. Flanders, it's Dwayne Perdue." The voice was thin and high over the hum of long distance. "My lawyers told me you want me to appear on your television show? I'm calling from Los Angeles."

"I'm glad you called, Mr. Perdue. We're doing a remote broadcast of the Sausalito town council meeting dealing with the closing of the Perdue Home due to the alleged infirmity of its members—"

"Oh yes, those poor women—"

"And naturally, of course, we want to get all points of view. There will be a screening from a documentary in progress about the subject, and I'm sure you'd want to appear."

"And will those arrangements you mentioned still hold?"

"Oh, yes. We'll handle the airfare, send a limo to the airport, and put you up in a suite at the Mark Hopkins." Zan waved Mark silent as he started to sputter.

"Well, all right."

"Wonderful. I'll have my secretary call you with the arrangements. I'm looking forward to meeting you." Zan hung up the phone and smiled triumphantly at Mark, her eyes sparkling. "We've got him. It's going to be quite a show."

"It's going to be quite an *expensive* show. A limousine? A suite at the Mark Hopkins?"

"Oh Mark, don't be petty. We do that, and more, for the latest pubescent heartthrob in purple satin and sequins, just to get an interview."

"And who said we could show a clip from Stu's documentary?"

"Oh, didn't I mention that to you?"

Mark stood up. "When I said I'd give you a free hand with this, I didn't expect you to run with it quite this far. You're really enjoying this, aren't you? You're turning into Mike Wallace right before my eyes. Oh well, as long as the ratings hold up. They've been terrific."

"At least somebody noticed," Zan grumbled under her breath.

Mark threw a wave over his shoulder as he headed out the door. "Of course I've noticed. I'm getting a lot of credit for this, you know."

Zan laughed as she turned back to her typewriter. She already felt more cheerful after talking to Dwayne. Wait until Stu heard she'd gotten hold of him and he was going to appear on the show. Plus a clip from Stu's documentary would be on the air as well. He wouldn't be able to remain silent any longer; he'd finally have to admit he was pleased.

Claude Craven had large blue eyes as glassy as marbles. Someone must have told him that they were his best feature, for he blinked them at Zan with a limpid self-consciousness that set her teeth on edge. The briskness of Stu's blue gaze was like being knocked over by a cold wave, but Claude's slightly goggle-eyed stare merely made her long to shake him. Zan decided that she was getting rather tired of these "dates."

While she reassured Claude about the upcoming interview her eyes roamed the restaurant in search of Stu. The task was made difficult by the restaurant's design. Built on several levels staggered for privacy, it was hard to tell where Stu had gone to tape pick-up shots of the spare high-tech decor. Monochromatic tones of black and gray were broken up only by a pink neon sign on one wall proclaiming the restaurant's name, If You Knew Sushi. Long plastic channels filled with water spiraled down from the top level past each table. Bobbing on the bright blue water were tiny plywood boats, each filled with a selection of different sushi. The customers simply picked and chose which morsels they preferred.

Zan watched a bright orange piece float by. She usually preferred her fish broiled, with a little fresh lemon; she'd never been particularly fond of sushi. Tonight just the thought of having to eat it gracefully on camera was making her feel slightly queasy.

"Can't wait to eat," Claude confided. "You'll love the sushi here. I got into this place the first week it opened, you know. Took two and a half hours to get a table." He made it sound like a great accomplishment.

"Terrific," Zan replied weakly.

"I have to confess I was a bit torn as to which restaurant to suggest for my favorite date. You know *Mesquite*! has a three hour wait for a table now. And they have the best grilled capon with goat cheese and kiwis I've had yet. Maybe we should have gone there." He looked worried.

"Oh no, Claude, this will be perfect. Sushi is fine."

He brightened. "Yes, it's always right, isn't it? It's a modern classic, don't you agree?"

Zan was saved from having to answer by the arrival of Faye. She swept in dressed in a sleek red dress and a black lace scarf Zan had given her, towering at least four inches above her date, Max Herman.

"Sorry we're late, darling," she apologized, pecking Zan on the cheek. "Traffic, you know. You remember Max?"

"Of course." Zan introduced Max and Faye to Claude, and stole a look over their heads to scan the crowd for Stu.

While Max struck up a conversation with Claude, waving an unlit cigar to punctuate his remarks, Zan quickly told Faye about Dwayne's upcoming appearance. "Oh darling, how marvelous. You *are* a wizard. Of course Dwayne couldn't resist the limo and the suite; he's such a snob. And I'm sure we'll just roll right over him at the council meeting. Won't Stu be thrilled?"

"Yes, won't he."

Faye leaned in closer. "What do you think of this dress? Thank heaven all the old styles are in again, or else the three of us would have nothing to wear except our shabby little gardening outfits. I wore this in 'Danger Calls From Rio.' Max loves it. Isn't he adorable? I adore short men; they have such energy. Of course, it's not exactly a *coup de foudre*, like Bertie and Gaston or you and Stu, but it will do nicely, I think."

"Me and Stu?"

Faye drew back and looked at Zan. "Why darling, what's going on with you two? For heaven's sake, haven't you settled things yet?"

"What things?"

Faye shook her head, exasperated. "Well, I can understand things *dragging* a bit, perhaps, Stu can be such a bear, but haven't you pushed him a little bit?"

"Pushed Stu?"

"Well, not so he knows it, of course. You're not going to let that big beautiful man get away, are you?"

"Am I?"

"Hmmph." Faye shrugged thin shoulders. "With that attitude, you are. I can see you need a little help. Now you know how much I adore you, but Zan, forgive my saying this, but you seem a little thick about this issue, darling. It's that blasted innocence of yours, no, don't stop me, you know it's true. I can see I just have to take you under my wing. Now, here's what you do..."

Zan leaned closer to hear what fascinating advice the sophisticated Faye could give her, but just then she saw Stu lumbering toward them with Jack in tow.

He looked her up and down, his eyes taking in every inch of her creamy knit dress with matching cardigan. It was elegantly styled but it clung to every curve, and Zan felt a ripple of satisfaction at finally piquing Stu's interest.

When he brought his gaze back to her face he saw her watching him and turned quickly to Jack. "We'll have to adjust the lights again for that dress."

She stifled the urge to scream and instead trotted after Stu as he headed back toward the second level. "Hey, wait up. I've got something to tell you about."

Stu reached the alcove where they were to hold the interview and began fiddling with the lights. "What's that?"

"I got Dwayne Perdue on the show. The remote we're going to do at the town council meeting."

Stu looked at her, startled. "You found Dwayne? How?"

"I've heard a couple of stories about him as a young boy from Amelia, Bertie and Faye. They knew him pretty well. I thought a greedy little boy would probably turn into a man who might be seduced by a limousine and a suite at the Mark Hopkins for the weekend. I left a message with his lawyers a week ago, and he called this morning."

"I see." Stu bent down to the lights again.

"I also," Zan went on doggedly, "got permission to show your entire documentary at the town meeting. They liked the clip so much, you know," she said innocently, and grinned when Stu shot her a sour look. "And Mark has agreed to show a clip on 'Modern Times on Screen.' I'll let you choose the tape this time, though."

"Thanks a lot."

"Don't mention it. Anyway, the show should be pretty dramatic."

Stu picked up his camera. "That remote is our last show, right? In two weeks?"

She nodded.

"I should be able to get something together to show by then. Jack, hand me that cable, will you?" He turned back to Zan. "Can you sit over there and pick up a piece of sushi for me? I want to frame some shots. Jack will be shooting with a second camera over there, don't forget. Good, here come the others."

Zan nodded and went over to sit where he had indicated. She was surprised she didn't disintegrate with the force of her fury. What did it take to hear Stu say, "Good job, Zan"? Winning the Nobel Peace Prize?

Stu bent behind the camera. "Pick up the sushi, okay? I want to get that silly boat in the picture."

She reached for the least offensive morsel she could find and nibbled at it experimentally.

"Mmmmm, I just adore the eel eggs," Claude said approvingly.

Zan coughed and took a long sip of water. She looked over the rim of her glass and saw Stu grinning his crinkly-eyed, chipped-tooth, maddening grin.

"Darling, you look pale," Faye said.

"At least your face matches your dress," Stu pointed out.

"Just shoot, Temple, don't editorialize," Zan responded.

"Testy, testy." Stu bent behind the camera again.

She turned to Faye, Max, and Claude. In the past weeks she'd learned that the best method of conducting the interviews was to get them off to a fast start.

"Do you think all this new emphasis on food is a substitute for sex?" she asked brightly.

The three excitedly began to talk at once, and Zan seized the opportunity to slip her remaining eel eggs into her napkin. It turned out to be such a good technique that she continued to smoothly dump a piece in her lap whenever the discussion reached an excited pitch, which, owing to the decided opinions of Max and Faye and the sputterings of Claude, tended to happen frequently. By the time it was over, she had a napkin full of unidentifiable marine animals and a slight headache.

"Okay folks, it's a wrap. Thanks a lot," Stu said, shutting off his camera.

Zan carefully crumpled her napkin and put it on the table, mentally wincing for the busboy who would find it. She chatted with Faye for a minute about the success of the taping, and when Faye, Max and Claude said goodbye she stood for a moment and then sank back into her chair after they piled down the stairs, still arguing and chattering.

Stu was talking to Jack, his camera still on his shoulder, and Zan took the opportunity to watch him unobserved. He was so handsome. There was so much of him she wanted, so much of him she liked. But there was so much of him she didn't understand, and was so afraid to try.

Jack nodded several times at Stu and turned to strike the lighting equipment. Zan got up to help him.

"Good show," he said as she approached. "Best yet."

"Thanks." Zan wound a cord around her arm grumpily. At least Jack noticed when things went well.

"Next week we have the croquet game with all the men who've been on the series and the three crazy ladies. Can't wait. The show's doing so great, everybody's talking about it. Even Stu has to admit that its been good publicity for him."

"Oh really? Did he say that?"

"Nah. I'm sure he's thinking it, though. Not that he needs it."

"Well, he might get some more jobs out of it."

"Oh, he doesn't need the jobs, or the money. He can pick and choose his projects."

"Oh," Zan said, confused. She'd been under the impression that Stu had agreed to work on this for the money. Maybe he gave a brighter picture to Jack of his financial situation than what really existed.

"For instance," Jack went on, "this next project he's had in the works for a year now. These folks in Hollywood are offering to finance the entire thing. It's a hot topic—a counterterrorism squad. He's already gone through months of negotiations with the actual squad in the Middle East. Even I don't know where they are."

"And he's already gotten the financial backing?"

"Sure, if he wants it. Then there's this other production company that wants him to do some feature film, but of course he's refused. Says it's incredible how much the price goes up every time he says no. But of course he'd only direct that film, not produce it. He'd never go for that. Besides, it's not a documentary. This Middle East thing, though. Wow. Can't wait. Here, let me take that cable."

"So the terrorism film is his next project."

"I expect so. Hasn't finalized anything, but it's just a question of time. Then we're off to the Middle East somewhere for about a year or so."

"A year or so?"

"Oh, yeah, it's an extensive project. A dream assignment."

"A dream assignment," Zan repeated hollowly. She leaned against the railing as Jack finished packing the equipment. Why hadn't Stu told her of his plans?

Why should he tell you? a rational voice responded. What was she to him? Why should he suddenly break his record for tight-lipped silence on all important matters just because he could be leaving the country at some point for a year or more to make a little lightweight documentary on counterterrorism? Why should he discuss his decision with a woman who made video documentaries on dating in the 80's?

In a stiff angry silence, she drove home with Stu, her head pounding. He seemed not to notice, driving swiftly through the dark streets of the city toward the bridge. The moonless night fell around them like a cloak that held no warmth, and as they drove across the bridge Zan looked back across the black water at the city retreating behind them. It sparkled and shimmered in the brisk cool air, holding out promises of glittering romance.

She wrenched her head away to concentrate instead on the dark hills of Marin County waiting to envelop them. For once, the sight of them did not comfort her. It seemed she was traveling away from bright possibilities to dark lonely destiny, and she was in no more control of her journey than she was in the driving of Stu's car.

She felt bruised and battered by emotions she couldn't sort out, and when Stu pulled up in front of her house she couldn't bear to look at him. She said good-night quickly and swung open the door with fierce energy, then slammed it with the same force.

Stu got out and looked at her, puzzled. "Something bothering you?"

"No. Good night." She started up the walk.

He followed, and she spun around angrily, nearly knocking him off balance. "You don't have to walk me to my door. I'm not helpless."

"I know that." When she turned, he continued to follow.

She spun around again, and he shrugged. "It's almost midnight," he pointed out mildly, "and I want to see you inside. Just let me do it, all right?"

They stomped up to the door in silence. Zan was afraid to look at Stu; if he had that faint knowing smile on his face that he'd been wearing lately she'd surely turn homicidal. She fumbled in her purse for her keys.

"It was a good interview tonight, Zan. We can edit it into a great segment."

She turned to face him slowly as her anger ticked off long seconds. "Excuse me, Stu, but I think I may have just heard a positive remark pass your lips. I should send a transcript to Ripley's Believe It Or Not. Mr. Stewart Temple, who's gone for thirty-five years without giving a compliment. You'd be a big hit at county fairs— They could put you right next to the two-headed cow!"

Stu raised his eyebrows. "Ah, I didn't realize you were so insecure. I didn't know you needed to be flattered constantly."

"Insecure!" she sputtered. "No, I just happen to be a normal human being instead of an emotionless robot."

Stu grinned. "Zan, you're looking especially lovely this evening," he said grandly, "the positive picture of pulchritude—"

"And you," she said, advancing on him angrily, "are the picture of pretentiously smug smiling superiority." Stu's grin only got wider, and Zan's bottled-up frustration exploded. "Will you just go away and leave me alone?" she yelled. "I don't want you in my life." She grabbed him by his tie and pulled him down to within inches of her face, her eyes blazing. "I don't want you," she said ferociously. "Oh God, I don't want you..." She pulled him down closer, and their mouths met in a crazed, inflammatory kiss. It was fast and furious, aching, raging.

Finally, finally she could explore him. Her hands could range over his back and shoulders and feel their strength; she could caress the dusky smoothness of his hair. Under his hands her body blazed into life, and she welcomed it. She felt as though she'd been parched forever and cool spring water was trickling down her throat.

When they broke apart Stu kissed her everywhere, her nose, her eyebrows, her ear, the line of her jaw, all the while murmuring roughly, "I've been waiting so long for that. Too long. Too long..." His fingers twined through her hair and tilted her head back so that his eyes could search hers. "I wanted you to come to me. I didn't think I'd have such a hard time waiting. I'm not a patient man."

"And you don't play fair," she said hoarsely.

He kissed her neck. "No, Zan, I don't play fair."

She reached up and held his head against hers for an instant. "Let's go inside."

She unlocked the door with unsteady hands and Stu followed her into the living room. They stood in the middle of the room awkwardly for a moment.

"I'll light a fire," Zan finally said. "Why don't you take off your jacket and get comfortable."

She shrugged off her own jacket and crossed to the fireplace. Kicking off her pumps, she knelt and laid a fire with hands that still shook slightly. She rocked back on her heels and held out cold fingers to the flickering orange flames. When Stu came and lowered himself next to her he took her hands between his own to warm them. His shirt was now open at the collar and she gave in to an urge to run her finger along the few hairs she could glimpse at the opening.

He pulled her down so that they were lying side by side in front of the fire. His eyes were liquid and dark, stirring her with their intensity. His face was beautiful to her, the fair skin, the wide mouth, the straight dark march of his eyebrows. She ran her finger over the bump on his nose and the chip in his front tooth. Even his imperfections only made him infinitely more desirable, more precious.

He cupped her face in his hands and studied it in return. "What color are your eyes?" he asked, his expression absorbed. "I've asked myself that question over and over, when I see you in different lights, in different moods. Are they amber or hazel? Light brown or mossy green? The color of honey or sunlight through trees?" His thumbs smoothed her cheekbones. "All I know is that they're the loveliest I've ever seen. And the warmest."

He brought her face closer and kissed her deeply, slowly, letting the flickers of arousal in her build until the force of her desire took her by surprise. His tongue explored her mouth and the sweet taste of him drugged her into a hazy wild confusion. His mouth and hands were everywhere, demanding everything, and she gave herself up to their power. When his fingers slipped underneath her skirt to caress her thigh and went still higher, she arched up against him with a soft cry.

His hand went flat against her for an instant, waiting. When she moaned and rocked against it, his fingers moved softly in a tantalizing, rhythmic dance, coaxing a response from her rigid body. Heat built up and sent her muscles thrumming; she arched even higher, straining, trembling, and the heat suddenly splintered into a million tiny fragments. Her body shook, and she collapsed against his chest.

Something within her, some cold center she had harbored for so long, began to crack and melt, spinning out rivers of warmth throughout her body, smooth and golden like brandy. She gripped Stu's shoulders and hid her face against him, feeling sudden tears scorch her cheeks.

His hands were still moving, stroking her, one on her trembling thigh, one on her hair. When the hot tears finally slid onto his neck, he moved away, startled, to gaze into her face. Zan only burrowed deeper into his neck as the tears flowed faster. Heavy sobs racked her, and though she tried to get control of herself with a series of shuddering breaths, she only cried harder. It seemed she would never stop, could never stop, and she was grateful for the soft light of the room and Stu's hard shoulder.

His touch immediately abandoned passion for tenderness. He hugged her gently. "Shhhh," he soothed, his voice low and honeyed. "It's all right, sweetheart. Everything's all right."

Zan continued to cry on his already drenched shoulder. She had no idea why she was crying but she couldn't stop, and though her sobs lessened, the tears still flowed. She cuddled against Stu, comforted by soft words and gentle hands.

"I'm sorry," she hiccuped into his shoulder. "I don't know why I'm doing this."

"It's all right, love."

"I'm so embarrassed."

"Don't be."

"I got your shirt all wet. It's wrinkled."

"It's okay. I've recently heard of the concept of dry cleaning."

Zan giggled into his chest, then looked up at him. "That's never happened to me before," she said softly.

"Hysteria in the middle of a passionate encounter?"

"No, the rather intense passion before the hysteria."

"Ah." His hands soothed her tense shoulders. He bent down to whisper in her ear. "You'd better get used to it."

"Oh, Stu." Zan felt her lower lip tremble through her smile, and another tear slid down her cheek. "I feel... I don't know what I feel, so many things, but mostly right now I feel embarrassed."

"Zan." He hugged her fiercely. "If you say that again I'm going to feel really insulted."

She snuggled closer, feeling the comforting rumble in his chest when he spoke. He twined his fingers through hers. "I want you to feel safe with me," he said. "We've started something tonight, and I want you to know that what's happening between us has shaken me up just as badly as you. I take it very seriously. Do you believe me?" he asked roughly.

"I believe you," she whispered.

His hand tightened on hers. "We're like this," Stu said, holding up their entwined fingers. "Trust that. Trust me. Do you?"

"I trust you."

"Good." He settled her more firmly against him, tucked her head underneath his chin, and by the light of the flickering fire, they slept.

Zan nestled deeper into the soft quilt to shield her eyes from the morning light. When she felt a hard surface underneath her hip, she opened one eye and remembered that she wasn't in her bed after all, but was curled up on the Oriental rug in her living room. But the body that had curled up around her during the long night was no longer there.

She sat up and surveyed the room sleepily. She remembered falling asleep in Stu's arms; she remembered a pillow being put under her head and a quilt tucked around her; she remembered Stu slipping her dress and pantyhose off to leave her in her short slip. Most of all, she remembered being held by strong arms the whole night long. What a strange, warm, wonderful night it had been. She had slept next to Stu as contentedly and as chastely as a child.

It hadn't been a dream, but what had happened to Stu? Zan finally fixed her bleary eyes on a slip of paper taped to the mantlepiece. She got up to read it.

I am severely restraining myself at this very moment from climbing back under that quilt and waking you up in a very unorthodox but delightful manner. Instead, I am going to be a responsible adult and go to my breakfast meeting.

Besides, I think you need some time to adjust to this new development. That's okay. We have all the time in the world. Why don't you throw on some clothes and meet me at my office around eleven? I'll treat you to the best brunch San Francisco has to offer.

Yours, Stu

Still holding the paper, Zan slowly walked up the stairs to the shower. It was obvious that Stu was thinking of them as a couple, that last night had changed something for both of them. They would no longer dance around each other, denying their attraction. She had been stripped vulnerable to him last night, and perhaps he was a man to value that. She reached over thoughtfully to turn on the hot water in the shower full blast and perched on the edge of the tub while the bathroom filled with steam. Obviously it was time for their relationship to go forward to the next step. Stu was expecting it, and her behavior last night had certainly indicated that she wanted it.

She was twenty-nine years old; she was no longer an innocent. But she had been mistaken once before, and the results had been disastrous. It had taken her so long to recover from the pain of Todd's infidelity, the casual attitude she had discovered in him about their commitment. Afterward, her friends had haltingly confided that they hadn't been surprised, and that fact had shocked her even more than Todd's betrayal. How could she have so misread him? How could she have been so blind as to think that she could have ever been happy with him? The only conclusion, for Zan, had been to assume that love was, after all, blind, and that she was particularly vulnerable to its dangers. Her response was to resolve not to take it seriously, and it had worked. She made a good living from her column, and up till now had been perfectly content to remain alone in her bed, making suitably droll comments on the situation.

Could she continue to keep that distance and have Stu too? Could she sleep with him and not feel the need to explore the depth of his commitment to her? And what of his next project? Would he agree to the assignment and then disappear to halfway around the world in a few months? They would have to enter into the relationship already knowing its limits. Didn't accepting that go against everything she knew about herself? Zan leaned over to temper the hot water with cold, and a needle of sharp fear shot through her at the thought of what lay ahead.

I won't worry about it now, Zan told herself, wiggling out of her slip. She'd take a shower, dress, and catch the ferry to the city, then walk to Stu's office and kiss him hello with every bit of the tenderness she felt for him. Beyond that moment, she would not consider. She stepped into the now cold shower and shivered at the shock.

Chapter Nine

The brisk breeze and bright blue sky on her ferry ride across the bay chased away any unpleasant thoughts. It was hard to worry about the future in such a glorious present. Zan sat on the top level, exposed to the wind and sky. She inhaled the steam from her hot coffee gratefully and tilted her head back on the seat to catch the sun's rays as the gleaming white city grew closer.

She had dressed for the cool weather in trim black pants tucked into soft leather ankle boots and a bulky blue-green wool sweater. The yellow wool scarf she'd added for extra warmth made her feel sunny and cheerful. She returned the wide smile of the ferry operator as he unfastened the barricade and ushered her onto the gangplank with a wave. Zan practically danced across it.

The clock tower at the Ferry Building told her she had plenty of time to walk to Stu's office, but she found herself half-running, suddenly impatient to see him. She swung south off Market Street and quickened her pace even more when she saw the large converted warehouse that housed Stu's office. The building was quiet; Zan supposed that even the various dedicated filmmakers and designers who had offices there couldn't resist this sunny Saturday.

Stu's office door was still locked, so she balanced on the railing and reached up on the sill above the door to find the key. If Stu knew he might be late for their meetings, he would hide it there for her. Zan found it and jumped down to open the door. She turned on the lights, smiling at the usual chaos.

"Hiya, Mooch," she greeted the fish, who regarded her balefully from his glass bowl. She opened the filing cabinet to get the fish food and found a note taped to the small container.

> I knew you couldn't resist Mooch's soulful look. I cued up the tape from last night if you want to take a look at it while you wait. I'm calling it The Great Sushi Sneak. Miss me yet?
>
> Still yours, Stu

Smiling, Zan fed Mooch, then crossed to the editing console. She sank into a chair and pressed play. The high-tech design of If You Knew Sushi appeared on the screen, and then a moment later the camera zoomed in on her. Zan laughed out loud as she watched herself sweep a piece of sushi into her lap with a guilty expression. She'd been so proud of that sly move, and Stu had caught it after all.

As a matter of fact, he'd caught every sneakily dumped piece, she discovered as she watched the rest of the tape. Zan had to admit that it made an amusing counterpoint to the discussion, which was a sometimes heated battle about modern trends between Claude and Faye and Max.

She laughed again as Claude made a point about new trends in food mirroring the attitudes of their generation, and Stu caught her nodding politely while sweeping eel and seaweed into her lap. As the discussion drew to a close, she realized why Stu had said it would be their best segment yet.

The screen went dark for a second or two, but before she could hit the stop button she appeared on screen again. Stu had continued taping after she'd thought he'd shut off the camera. The camera zoomed in to a closeup of her face as she talked to Faye, and kept it tightly framed as expressions flitted across it: laughter, wryness, affection. Then the lens focused on the tip of one finger and trailed up her arm, shoulder, neck, to focus on her face again, then make its leisurely way down the other shoulder, along her midriff, her slim hips in the knit dress, and began an excrutiatingly slow journey down her crossed legs.

The movement was like a caress; there was somehow a lyrical tenderness in the camera's scrutiny. Never before had her body been so lovingly detailed. It was slyly amusing and erotic all at once, and Zan flushed at this clearly documented evidence of Stu's desire.

The traveling lens stopped finally with a lingering closeup of the arch of her foot, daintily and circumspectly searching for her pump underneath the table. Her foot finally slid into it, the camera cut to a relieved smile on Zan's face, and then she turned slightly, apparently looking at something to the right of the camera. Zan watched the monitor as her eyes grew soft and—there was no other word for it—hungry.

She had been looking at Stu, she knew. She knew it was a classic documentary technique, to rest the camera on the shoulder, not looking through the viewfinder, but all the while having the subject expertly lined up in the lens. The unsuspecting subject would reveal more if they didn't know they were being filmed. Now, watching her face, the thought rushed through her mind before she could stop and analyze the picture. *I look like a woman in love.*

She shook her head and pushed the freeze frame button. Not love, surely not that. But she had to admit she appeared to be in the grip of some vast complicated feeling. Her frozen image stared back at her, eyes huge in a face taut with emotion. Could it be that Stu was confronting her with the evidence of her desire? He was showing her that she could no longer run from it; it was there, in all its naked simplicity, and they both knew it. No matter what the consequences, she could run from it no longer.

The phone rang suddenly, and Zan looked around. It wasn't in its usual place on top of Stu's desk, and she got up and searched under piles of papers while it rang. Finally she discovered the cord with a cry of satisfaction, and she began to follow it around chairs and equipment and tables. Scuttling after it frantically while the ringing went on, Zan emitted a howl of surprise when her head connected sharply with the edge of Stu's desk. She bounced back, landed in a convenient chair, and the phone stopped ringing. The answering machine clicked on.

Stu's voice calmly explained that he wasn't available but to please leave a message.

"Oh, shut up," Zan told his mechanical voice crossly.

"Stu, Scott Jones here." The disembodied voice was startlingly loud in the quiet office. "Just got back to the hotel from our meeting, and I wanted to say again how glad we are that you decided to come aboard. I already called Jerry Torbey re your concerns on the terrorism thing, security for your crew, and so on, and he agrees. No problem. We can set up something before you start shooting in three weeks. Again, glad you have no commitments and we were able to finalize the deal. See you in L.A. next week for the final meeting. We'll do lunch."

Zan heard the click of the answering machine shutting off with a terrifying acuteness. It was as though a mist had lifted from her eyes and revealed a shocking landscape. Her eyes lifted slowly to the image of herself, still frozen on the monitor. Her face stared back from the screen with its look of aching vulnerability.

"You fool," she told the innocent woman on the tape, and shut it off.

"Glad you have no commitments..." the man had said. No, Stu certainly didn't have any commitments, she knew that. One night spent sleeping next to her on her rather worn Oriental rug didn't count. Neither did two hands clasped together and a voice low with emotion telling her to trust that joining. Nor the promise *"We have all the time in the world..."*

How could Stu say such things, knowing he was leaving? How much time did they have? A few weeks before he got on a plane and flew away for a year or more? Was that what "time" meant to a documentarian—three weeks to explore a relationship, a year to explore danger and death?

Three weeks was plenty of time for an affair, just right, in fact. Zan told herself stonily that she wasn't being unreasonable. She didn't want to deny him his work; she just felt entitled to all the facts before she jumped into bed with him. She took it too seriously not to, and obviously Stu did not. He didn't give a second thought to beginning an affair before disappearing.

Wait a second. Zan mentally reined in her galloping thoughts. Perhaps Stu had just decided to finalize the deal this morning. It hurt her a bit that he could leave her sleeping, still warm from his body, and immediately agree to embark on such a long-term project, but she had to admit it would be insanity on her part to imagine that she could divert him from a course he'd been pursuing for months.

In that case, he would tell her about his decision when he arrived. He wouldn't urge her into bed without letting her know. And so they would just have to postpone their relationship. A hurdle remained ahead of her; she would have to refuse him now, and that would be painful, almost as painful as not seeing him for a year.

She knew she wouldn't be able to make love to Stu and then wave him onto a plane in a few weeks with a careless heart. Perhaps in a year, she would see him again, and then they could begin again. As for now, he'd agreed to the deal, and that was that. And he'd tell her when he came in. He would.

"Won't he?" she asked Mooch.

"Won't who what?" Stu asked, entering the room briskly.

"Won't you be here soon. I'm starved."

"Me too," Stu said, coming over and kissing her lightly. "I only had coffee at the meeting so I could stuff myself later in front of you."

"How considerate. So, how did your meeting go?"

"Fine." Stu took her hands and raised her up to stand next to him. "Give me a proper welcome, will you?" He kissed her softly, lingeringly, and when he pulled away he sighed by her ear and held her closer. "I've been thinking about doing that all morning."

"You couldn't have been very attentive at your meeting."

He kissed her ear. "I wasn't. It wasn't very important, though."

"Well, I hope you didn't agree to anything you'll regret, since you were so distracted."

Stu continued his tantalizing nibble on her lobe. "Oh, no. I try not to do anything I'll regret. That's probably why I managed to be so good last night. Today, however, is a different matter. Today, I have a feeling I'm going to be very, very bad."

His teeth nipped her ear and Zan stepped back with a shaky laugh. "I think we'd better feed you first. And me. And you can tell me all about your meeting."

"It was standard meeting material. Weak coffee, good Danish, which I resisted. You know, if you keep this up, I'm going to have to revise my opinion of myself as completely irresistible." He held out his index finger. "Care to sink your teeth into this again?"

"I'd rather have an omelette."

"I knew you were a woman of healthy appetites, but I hoped they occasionally strayed in a more interesting direction." He looked over her head at the editing console. "Did you watch the tape?"

"Yes."

He raised her chin with his finger so that she had to look at him. "And what did it tell you?"

"That I'd better be very, very careful."

"Is that all? Didn't it tell you how I feel? How you feel? How much I want you? How much you want me?" Zan felt her body liquify at the suggestive, heavy beat of his words. When he kissed her she met his embrace fiercely, wanting to forget her uneasiness, wanting to give in if only for a moment to the pulse that beat in her whenever he was near. Her desire hadn't diminished with the new day; it was still there, as clear and strong as morning sunlight.

They kissed for a long time, until her knees were weak and her mind confused. When they drew apart Stu clasped her to him tighter, his breathing ragged. "Oh God, Zan, I don't want to wait anymore."

"I don't either, Stu. I want to—"

"Come with me then." Stu took her hand and began to lead her to the back rooms of the office.

"Stu, no. I didn't mean..."

"Don't be shy, darling. You know that nice big couch you've taken naps on when we've worked late? It's pretty comfortable." He kissed her again. "Although since you can drive me wild on linoleum, I imagine that—"

"Stu, please wait. I want to ask you something."

He stopped. "All right," he said quietly. "What is it, Zan? What's bothering you?"

She felt uncomfortable, and the beginnings of anger stirred her. Why should she have to *ask* him? "Last night you said some things," she began. "About taking us seriously, about trust."

"And I meant them. Zan," he said softly, cradling her face in his hands, "I can't promise you anything except my honesty."

"Your honesty," she repeated dully.

"Yes. About how much I care for you." He held her gaze steadily. "We're going to make love. You know that. What does it matter if it happens now, or tonight, or next week or next month?"

"How about next year?"

Stu laughed as he picked up her hand and pressed his lips against the palm. "That might be difficult. I could never wait that long for you."

"You couldn't?"

"Not without going insane."

She turned around, afraid her anguish would show in her eyes. Stu reached around her from behind, his mouth against her cheek. "Don't say no. Make love to me now. Make love to me . . ."

Each urging went through her like a stab wound. "No!" she said suddenly, fiercely, and turned back around, breaking Stu's hold on her. His arms slid down and hung by his sides.

"I almost forgot," she continued, calmer now, "I have a—a deadline for my column. I have to work."

"And you forgot?" Stu asked carefully.

"It happens sometimes."

"Then we'll just have to have dinner tonight instead. I can do some work here, then pick you up at your office."

"No! I mean, I have to work tonight, too."

"Zan, is something—"

"Listen, Stu, I'd better go."

"Well, at least let me take you to breakfast first."

"I'm not hungry." Zan inched away toward the door, trying not to meet Stu's bewildered eyes. She desperately needed to be alone, and fast. "I'll call you, okay?"

He didn't answer. After one quick last look at him, she slipped out the door. Shutting it behind her softly, she flew down the stairs. When she pushed open the front door of the building, the beauty of the day was an affront. She shielded her eyes from the glare.

She took off briskly down the street, trying to ignore the disturbing voices inside her urging her to return, to run back up the stairs and throw herself back into Stu's arms. She was taking this all too seriously, the voices chided her. Stu wasn't obligated to tell her his every career move before taking her to bed. What was the big deal?

"It's a big deal to me!" Zan cried back silently to those voices. When she gave herself to a relationship again, it should have stability and potential for growth. She knew she couldn't stand it any other way. Embarrassing as it was to admit, the flip, caustic Zan Flanders was an old-fashioned, serious sap. When she'd calmed down, she'd just have to tell Stu that she wasn't ready to get involved with him after all. She wondered how badly that might make him feel. Or perhaps he'd simply be frustrated, and find someone else to relieve it during his last few weeks in San Francisco.

Her steps slowed as she remembered suddenly her last glimpse of Stu before she'd fled out the door. It had been a quick, anxious glance, but his image was burned into her brain. His expression had been disturbingly familiar, as if she had looked upon it once before. It slipped around the corners of her mind, teasing her, until she remembered. She inhaled sharply. That taut, aching look of vulnerability was identical to the expression on her own face in the close-up freeze frame she'd studied.

Zan walked grimly on to escape the implications of such a comparison. What did she know about looks of vulnerability and pain, anyway? All that had really been on their respective faces was a look of thwarted lust, nothing more.

She certainly wasn't about to feel sorry for Stu Temple. He had lied to her, a lie of omission that was no less pernicious than an outright untruth. He was perfectly willing to involve her in an affair without disclosing something about himself that she had every right to know. Simple lust had been the reason; he knew that she was the kind of woman to refuse intimacy knowing that their relationship could only have an uncertain future. Just as he'd said, he could not wait a year for her. How ironic that Stu, with all his offbeat, rumpled charm, had turned out to be a classic Bachelor of the 80's, after all.

Zan jumped when a hand descended on her shoulder. Turning quickly, she discovered Mark McFee behind her.

"Working on Saturday again?" he asked. "Are you angling for a promotion or something?"

She looked around, slightly dazed, and discovered that she was in front of the *Modern Times* offices. "Just thought I'd work a little on a new column," she told him, recovering quickly.

"I'm dutifully impressed, but you're still not getting a promotion. I'd probably have to give you my job."

The security guard waved them in and they got on the elevator together. "I don't want your job anyway," Zan said. "I'd find it boring to sit around and read the sports pages all day."

"Not all day," Mark said huffily. "I have lunch, too, you know. So how are things winding up with the video doc? That's short for documentary. Notice how easily I slipped in that jargon? Have to remember to try that on the executive producer."

"The doc is fine." The elevator came to their floor and they paused before going off in their separate directions.

"I guess Stu is getting antsy to go on to his next project," Mark said. "He'll have to pack a few automatic weapons with his camera this time. Counterterrorism—no fooling around with that one."

"You know about that?"

"Sure. Stu told me about it at the very beginning of this project. Wanted me to know that we couldn't extend the project past the projected time, since he'd be leaving for the Middle East. Didn't you know that?"

"Oh, sure." She kept her tone light.

"Buzz me later if you want to catch a bite. Otherwise I'll see you Monday. Okay?"

"Sure. So long, Mark." Zan headed for her office slowly, her anger building with each measured step. Even Mark had known for weeks about Stu's plans. Why had Stu kept them from her? Was it to manipulate her into bed? Or, more likely, was it simply because he didn't feel it was important? On a business level, he needed to tell only his employer and his assistant; on a personal level, there was nobody he needed to tell at all.

She paused in front of her office door. It had been no accident, she realized, that she'd ended up in front of the Modern Times Building today. Work had always been her shield and her remedy against hurt. There was no emotional distress she couldn't turn into an anecdote. It was why she'd turned to satire instead of fiction in the first place, after Brody's death and Todd's betrayal. She'd always preferred laughter to tears, lampooning to lamenting.

"Weep no more, Alexandra," she muttered, pushing open the door. "Write."

She savagely flipped on the office light and threw herself into her desk chair. Staring at the typewriter, she considered her options. She knew she couldn't publish a column about what happened to her with Stu; it would be an invasion of his privacy. But she could write one, and perhaps just the act of getting her murderous thoughts down on paper would calm her down. At least it might help her to be civil when she saw Stu again. Having already vented her anger, she might not be so tempted to shriek at him.

She rammed a piece of paper into the typewriter and stared at the blank sheet for several minutes. Then she haltingly tapped out, "The Bachelor of the 80's, Part Two: Or, Girls, Beware of Camouflage." The hesitant, irregular tap of the keys soon quickened as her anger translated into the soothing distance of irony.

The clarity of black ink on white paper helped her to organize the savage thrust of her thoughts. "Not every Bachelor of the 80's wears an Italian suit and drives a German car that he's in hock up to his eyebrows for," she wrote. "Some of them wear faded jeans and unraveling sweaters and drive wood-paneled station wagons that disarm you with their suburban innocence. But the tools of seduction are just an imaginative variation on an old theme: the artful romanticism of white lilacs; the charming simplicity of graham cracker ice cream; the carefully offhand admission that he bakes his own cookies. Don't be fooled—like the smooth Bachelor of the 80's' reliance on his expense account and his stereo system, this man is only offering teasing hints of his emotions. Experienced he may be, but he parcels out his feelings like a reluctant emotional virgin. He saves his true emotional commitment for his work and for himself. Women are too lightweight to fit into such a dedicated coupling."

She typed furiously for some time, occasionally staring out the window at the tiny slice of bay. By the time the shadows lengthened on the sidewalks down below, she was winding up. "It's lucky we're too smart to get taken in," she wrote. "But women have sensitive antennae when it comes to a man's ability to respect them. When he considers a confession that he 'cares' a giant step toward intimacy, how can you possibly take him seriously? It's a difficult prospect to get your arms around a man who's busy patting himself on the back."

"Remember girls," she finally concluded, "that with this man you definitely just want to have fun. Put on your red high heeled pumps and dance up a storm. But when he says 'trust me,' kick them off and run like hell. At least you won't have to ride around in that station wagon anymore."

Zan sat staring quietly at what she had written. She didn't feel soothed by the righteousness of her anger. She really didn't feel very much at all; the ache in her stomach was empty and hollow.

"You just need to eat something," she reassured herself out loud, but her voice carried no authority. She sighed wearily, turned off the typewriter, and left the office. She gave a forlorn wave to the security guard in the lobby as she left, but somehow she wasn't surprised when he didn't wave back.

Chapter Ten

The Sausalito town council meeting was packed this time, and it wasn't because of Howie the Clam. The people filing in through the oak doors and sitting down with an air of expectancy had all arrived for the predicted fireworks surrounding the vote on the Paradise Perdue Home for Retired Actresses closing.

Zan was aware of the rumors, since she'd been the one to start them. She'd decided that a noisy, enthusiastic crowd was absolutely necessary for what she'd cooked up with the members of the Home. She scanned the crowd and finally saw the members file in, along with the various "dates" Amelia, Bertie and Faye had had on "Modern Times on Screen." She grinned at Gaston and Max and waved at Sludge, who was sporting silver sparkles in his hair for the occasion.

She only wished she weren't so tired. The past two weeks had passed in a blur of hard work, so constant that she'd fallen into bed each night too exhausted to remain awake for more than a second or two. That was the way she'd wanted it; she didn't want to think, she only wanted to work. When she had time for leisurely thoughts, they always revolved around Stu.

It had been surprisingly easy to avoid seeing Stu alone over the past two weeks since she'd run out on him in his office. They'd done much of their communicating through their phone answering machines. It had been a stroke of lucky timing that Stu was working around the clock to finish "Paradise Lost," his documentary on the Perdue Home, and that she was putting in the same hours with arrangements for this last show in her series. They had communicated through Jack on their editing chores, and she had just kept promising that when the two projects were over they would talk. It had helped immensely when Stu had left for Hollywood for five days; she'd been so relieved she hadn't even been angry at the fact that he hadn't explained why.

But she knew her day of reckoning was at hand. Stu was coming straight to the meeting from the airport, and she knew he would want to talk after it. When he'd left last week after their taping of the final "date," a hilariously chaotic croquet game, his expression had been so grave during their hurried goodbye that she'd known his patience was wearing thin at her strange habit of avoiding him and pretending everything was fine.

Zan estimated that Stu only had about ten days or so to go before he left the country, so any confrontation they would have would be a final one. His business here would be completed after tonight. He'd finished editing down "Paradise Lost" to its final thirty-minute length, and it would be shown here tonight. Then a clip would be shown on "Modern Times on Screen," and the local public television station had scheduled it for early January. With any luck, tonight Dwayne would be as ineffectual here as he'd been in the earlier interview she'd taped with Jack for the show, and the women would be assured of being able to remain in the Home. All of the ends would be tied up, except for one.

Zan felt a quiver of alarm as the object of her thoughts strode through the door. She watched him stop and speak to Jack, who was already starting to tape the crowd. He scanned the room until he saw her, then threaded his way over to her. He was wearing what must have been a new navy blue sports coat, casually but beautifully tailored. Must be the Hollywood influence, Zan sniffed to herself. Was it possible that he had picked it out all by himself?

"Nice jacket," she said as he came up to her. "But whatever happened to the college sophomore look?"

"Hello Zan, I missed you too," Stu answered, scowling. "We have to talk."

"I know. Well, we have a few minutes before the meeting starts. I can tell you about how Dwayne's interview went."

"That's not what I meant."

"Oh. Okay, why don't you call me tomorrow, and we can—"

"No." He said the word softly, but it had a weight of composed finality about it that boded no argument. His fingers closed around her wrist. "Tonight. I'm tired of playing phone tag with you, Zan. I've been talking to your machine and your assistant for two weeks now." She tried to tug her wrist free, but his fingers tightened on it. "I want you too much to let you slip away from me. Don't think that answering machines and assistants can keep me from you."

Zan moistened her dry lips with the tip of her tongue. "You seem confident."

His fingers moved slightly to feel the pulse in her wrist. "I can feel your blood racing as we speak," he said. "I can feel you tremble when I touch you. Can you look into my eyes and tell me you don't want me too?"

His eyes held hers and she stood paralyzed by the certainty in them. Suddenly the gavel banged and she heard Janet Tibbles call the meeting to order. Stu dropped her wrist with a muffled curse and turned on his heel to join Jack at the rear of the room. She watched him until he had picked up a camera and positioned himself to film the proceedings. Only then could she move; she turned and saw Bertie waving her into a seat next to them.

She slid into it as Janet Tibbles began the meeting. "We're dealing with an unorthodox situation here," she said, "so we'll be proceeding in a rather unorthodox manner. Though since this is the city of Sausalito, I doubt many of you will notice this." She waited for the chuckles to die down before continuing. "This evening we must decide about the eventual fate of the Perdue Home. First we'll hear from Dwayne Perdue, then we'll see a short film, and finally we'll hear from the Home members themselves. Mr. Perdue, are you ready to speak to us?"

Flushed with self-importance and two days of room service at an exclusive hotel, Dwayne rose to go to the microphone at the front of the room. Zan found her attention wandering as he repeated, almost word for word, what he had told her on camera earlier in the day. Paradise had left no provision for the declining health and spirits of the members, and it was impossible for him to make the necessary improvements. He needed the city's agreement to change the provisions of the foundation, all for the good of, his eyes filling with tears, "those poor ladies."

Bertie leaned over to whisper at Zan. "I'm afraid Dwayne gets his acting ability from his mother," she said. "Poor Paradise never did know how to underplay."

"If you ask me, Paradise is rather lucky," Faye put in in a low tone. "She never had to see Dwayne grow up into such a horrid little man. It wasn't her fault he turned out so badly. She only had him for the summers, you know."

Dwayne finished his recital and made his modest way back to his seat as Jack went to the front of the room to introduce "Paradise Lost." The lights went out, and the documentary came on the large video screen. The first scene was of the croquet game of the week before, a wildly crazy affair punctuated by the shrieks of the three women and Zan as they battled each other and the other combatants in the game.

Zan was startled; she knew that up until two weeks ago Stu had chosen Livie's reminiscences for the first scene. But her astonishment only grew as the tape continued to play. She'd seen an early screening of the film and had been impressed and moved; it had been stark and powerful, focusing on the hardships of the women and the loss of Paradise's dream of security for them. Now the same scenes moved her, but they were lightened by the inclusion of outtakes from the "Modern Times on Screen" tapes. They were heartwarming and occasionally hilarious, and they shifted the focus of the film to the intense loyalty and camaraderie of the women, their wit and vitality in the face of their distress. As the audience laughed and murmured with pleasure, Zan discovered a surprising thing: Stu had made a touching, amusing, and very human film.

It ended with all the women reminiscing about Paradise while they watched a videotape of one of her old movies. There was a poignancy in their stories that brought tears to Zan's eyes, and it struck her anew how desperately she wanted to help them remain together. Glancing over, she saw Bertie take Faye's hand and squeeze it, and on the other side of Faye, Amelia did the same.

Touched by the women's gestures, Zan was brought up sharply when she returned her eyes to the screen as the credits came on. She was shocked when she saw her name flash on screen. "Produced by Zan Flanders and Stewart Temple," the credits read.

He had made her co-producer on his documentary. Zan gripped her hands together in her lap. After all his taunting, his teasing, he had decided that she'd made a significant enough contribution to the film to give her a credit he'd never allowed to anyone else. It was astounding and mystifying, and when the lights came back on she turned and searched the crowd for Stu. She found him leaning against a pillar, watching her coolly. Her puzzled eyes met his expressionless ones. Then he lifted his camera back to his shoulder as Dwayne got up to speak.

"It's just a film, and films can lie," Dwayne sputtered. "And actresses know that; they can create any kind of illusion they want. What about Olivia Grandee, who's in her eighties? My mother just didn't foresee these problems. She set up the foundation in a confused state of mind. These women don't need these anxieties! They need to rest!"

Zan poked Bertie and all the women stood up. "We are here to prove, once and for all," Bertie said in a high clear tone, "that we do not need rest. We just need

Dwayne to stop mismanaging funds so we can have money. We don't want to rest!"

From the front of the room, Sludge started a tape of "Limited Nuclear Love." Then he dashed back to escort the women to the front. As Gaston, Max, and assorted other escorts of the women came up front as well, they began an admirably orchestrated exhibition of break dancing. It was a little slow, and sometimes off the beat a bit, and Amelia never could quite master the moon walk, but it succeeded in completely delighting the audience. Despite the bangs from the gavel, the spectators went wild. Soon more people streamed up the aisle to join the fun.

When the music finally stopped, everyone stopped wiggling and jumping and turned to the council with expectant faces. Without further ado, they voted to reject Dwayne's propositions and to further look into the managing of the foundation. The audience cheered, and the council members came down to be congratulated on their popular decision.

Zan dashed up the aisle in search of Stu. She bumped into Jack instead, and she threw her arms around him. "We did it!" she cried. Stu materialized from behind Jack's back and she stepped forward awkwardly, suddenly shy.

"Congratulations, Stu," she said.

He nodded. "Same to you."

"You made me co-producer on your film. Why?"

He ran his fingers through his hair wearily. "Because you deserved it. You showed me in a thousand ways how to change the focus of the film and make it work. That last scene was pure Zan. Remember that day you told me I should have filmed the women watching Livie's old movie? You were right. That's why I went and rented one of Paradise's old films." He stopped and looked down at his camera for a moment. When he looked up again, his eyes were solemn. "You know I agreed to work with you because I wanted publicity for the Perdue Home. But I think there was another reason. I think somehow I sensed that you could give me something I'd been lacking in my work. That's probably why I was so nasty in the beginning," he admitted with a grin. "I have a hard time coming to terms with the fact that I can't do everything myself. But I've changed," he said softly. "You've changed me. My work will be different from now on, and that's because of you."

Zan looked away from him, confused. Never before in her life had she been beset with so many contradictory emotions. Her fantasy had come true, after all. Stu did respect her, more than she'd ever dreamed or was able to imagine. But now she realized that his professional respect fell far short of everything she'd been afraid to admit she was hoping for. The respect she craved was far more personal; it was respect for the feelings they had aroused in each other, respect for their seriousness and their permanency.

Pride finally made her raise her head. "Thank you, Stu," she said quietly. "I appreciate that."

He nodded rapidly. "I've been wanting to tell you that, but I decided that the film could say it better. But there's something else I have to tell you. Something important."

Fear made her stammer and withdraw. Suddenly, she wasn't ready to hear what he was finally ready to tell her. "I . . . I'm supposed to go celebrate with the ladies."

"Is that more important to you?"

"It's not that, but I—"

"Zan! Stu!" Amelia, Bertie and Faye descended on them with hugs, kisses, and exclamations. A gush of compliments followed about Stu's documentary.

"What a picture!" Faye said. "You know, Stu, when you showed us that clip weeks ago, it was rather grim, I must say. Very much like our lives of course, before darling Zan stepped in and shook everything up. Dates with industrialists—"

"Wine growers," Bertie said, her arm through Gaston's.

"Retired actors, an astrophysicist, a gambler—" Amelia put in.

"Now Amelia, shush, he might hear you, and anyway Max is not a gambler. He's a . . . a venture capitalist."

"Oh come *on*, Faye."

"Well, at least he's amusing. Now you two, we're all going to celebrate at that very tacky cocktail lounge across the street, so come on." She linked her arm through Zan's.

Stu held Zan's gaze all through the women's chatter. "Are you going?" he asked.

Faye looked from one to the other, and then disengaged herself from Zan. "Oh, Zan doesn't have to come, it's quite all right, you stay here with Stu, darling," she urged.

"No, Faye, I'll come with you," Zan said, turning to her. She couldn't bear Stu's eyes any longer.

"Well, all right, if you really think . . . All right, Amelia, we're ready, do stop tugging at me. Shall we go, girls?"

Zan joined the noisy confusion of their exit with relief. Stu had wanted her to stay behind, she knew; his eyes had told her that in no uncertain terms. She knew she was only postponing the inevitable, but she couldn't bear to hear him tell her he was leaving. There was time enough tomorrow to deal with the consequences of that; tonight was reserved for whatever half-hearted attempt at celebration she could muster up.

The clock read seven-thirty-two a.m., so why was the telephone ringing? Zan groaned when she tried to lift her head from the pillow. The last thing she remembered was falling into bed after bidding Amelia, Bertie and Faye good-night at their door and then paying a wildly exorbitant taxi fare at hers. A crushed pink paper parasol on the pillow next to her disheveled hair was an annoyingly bright reminder of their celebration at Gordo Flip's Polynesian Paradise Bar (Tropical Drinks Our Specialty).

Who could be calling her this early on a Saturday? She sat up groggily, and the pain in her head caused her breath to explode in a sharp hiss. A Zombie's Revenge might taste like coconuts and mangoes, but it packed quite a wallop. Falling back on the bed, she crawled to the edge and reached for the phone on her night table.

"This better be good," she whispered into the receiver.

"Zan? Is that you?"

"Mark." Zan slumped back against the pillows. "Why are you calling me before the sun is up?"

"You told me you were getting up early today. Whenever I wait to call you at a decent hour, you've already left."

"Mark, little Polynesian men with hammers are setting up shop inside my head. What do you want?"

"I wanted to tell you it was dynamite. The best! I've been getting great reactions from the rest of the staff already."

"Glad to hear it. What are you talking about?"

"Your latest column, sweetie. Wake up. We should start a whole new controversy."

"Terrific. Now, if you don't mind—"

"'Girls, Beware of Camouflage'! I love it!"

The dim clamoring in her brain became a roar. "What did you say?"

"'...difficult to get your arms around a man who's patting himself on the back...' Hah! I really laughed that day I got it off your desk. Meant to tell you, but you haven't been around lately."

"You got it off my desk?" Zan pressed her hand to her throbbing temples. She hadn't thrown it out? How could she have been so careless? And she'd been so wrapped up in her work and her avoidance of Stu that her assistant had been looking at the proofs of her column for her. Frantically, she tried to remember if she'd said anything in the column that could link it to Stu.

"That wood-paneled station wagon was a great touch," Mark said, chortling.

"Mark, thanks for calling, I've got to go now, bye." The words came out in a rush and Zan slammed down the phone without waiting for Mark's reply.

Horrified, she threw the covers back and sprang to her feet, looking wildly around to try to decide on a plan. Get dressed was first. Then buy up every copy of *Modern Times* in Sausalito and move on to San Francisco and Los Angeles. Or maybe she could drive over to Stu's and prepare him. The magazine had just hit the stands yesterday; he couldn't possibly have seen it already, could he?

She splashed some cold water on her face and pulled on a pair of faded jeans. She reached for a sweater and bounded down the stairs to the living room. Snatching her keys from the coffee table, she ran to the front door and flung it open. She nearly screamed when she encountered Stu Temple on her doorstep.

Zan opened her mouth to say something when she noticed that he was clenching a copy of *Modern Times* in his fist. She stepped back without a word and he advanced into the room.

"I did some interesting reading this morning," he began, his voice low.

"Stu, I—"

"Don't say anything, Zan. I don't think I could stand to hear you speak."

Her mouth snapped shut, effectively silenced by the contempt in his tone. He held up the magazine in front of her face and she closed her eyes for a second against the bold headline, the words she'd never dreamed would be printed.

"Is this what I am to you?" Stu demanded, his face taut with anger. "*Material?* A joke, an anecdote, a bit? Do you enjoy that? Do you? Do you enjoy turning a relationship into a one-liner?"

Zan turned away. "Stu stop! I didn't mean for the article to get published."

He stopped for a second and studied her through narrowed eyes. "What does that mean?"

"Mark found it on my desk and somehow it—"

"But you wrote it?"

She nodded.

"You wrote it that day you left me in my office, didn't you? This was that column you couldn't wait to write. It was that day, wasn't it?" When she didn't answer, he grabbed her arm and hissed fiercely, "Wasn't it?"

"Yes! But I thought—"

"I don't care what you thought!" Stu looked down at her arm, reddening from his grasp, and dropped it quickly. "Oh God," he groaned, and looked down at the floor while several long seconds passed. "You laid here with me all night long," Stu said, still looking at the floor, "and then went to your office that next day and wrote this. You didn't take us seriously for a moment."

And what about you, Stu? Zan asked silently. *You left here and finalized a deal that would take you from me for an entire year. And you never told me. How can you pretend to have taken us seriously at all?*

She swallowed hard against the lump in her throat. "Stu, I'm sorry that article got published. All I can say is that it was as much of a surprise to me as it was to you. I...I was trying to work things out in my head, put things in perspective—"

He looked up, and the expression in his eyes chilled her to the bone. The anguish was gone. Difficult as that had been to face, the sardonic bitterness she saw now was worse. He held up the magazine again. "And this is how you put everything in perspective, isn't it? By ridiculing it. When are you going to face it, Zan? Your life, your ex-fiancé, your brother's death—"

"Stop!" she whispered, color draining from her face. "Please stop."

Stu flung the magazine against the fireplace and it slithered to the floor. "All right," he said tiredly. "No more."

Zan reached out one hand to him but dropped it before it touched his sleeve. "Stu." Her voice came out hoarse and cracked. "It was a mistake."

He didn't look at her; he just turned away. "You bet it was," he said shortly, his voice sounding as strained as hers had been. He was gone before she could say another word.

Chapter Eleven

White lilacs? Are you crazy, lady?" The street vendor shook his head. "This is *November*, here. Take some mums instead, they're gorgeous. I'll throw in the bunch of autumn leaves, you make a nice arrangement, seven-fifty all together."

"No, thanks." Zan turned up the collar of her raincoat and prepared to duck out of the booth back into the rain. The sudden, silly, inexplicable urge for white lilacs had hit her while walking to her car from her office. She didn't know what she'd been thinking; she really didn't want the darned things anyway. She turned to go.

"Hey lady, you might try Les Fleurs du Coeur on Grant. You can probably get them there, if you're willing to pay. Or you could forget the flowers and buy a condo for what they charge."

"Thanks." It was ridiculous; she'd have to dodge through five blocks of savage and unprincipled rush hour umbrella-wielders to get there. Then she'd have to shell out a week's salary for the delicate out-of-season flowers and sprint back to the car with them mangled and dripping under her arm. It would take her twenty minutes to complete the errand, provided she was foolish enough to consider it.

It took her twenty-two minutes. At least the lilacs weren't too crushed, and she tossed them on the passenger seat with a sigh. The constant rain had snarled rush hour traffic even worse than usual, and she had to drive carefully, praying that the car would forgo its finicky nature in the rain and get her home in good time.

She had to inch across the Golden Gate Bridge along with a mass of commuters. In the middle, the line of cars stopped dead. Zan picked up the bouquet next to her and buried her nose in the fragrant flowers. She had to close her eyes against the sudden rush of pain as a vivid picture of Stu flashed through her mind as he'd looked that day in her garage, handsome and vital, dissipating the gloom of the day.

It had been so long since she'd allowed herself to picture him, clear and fresh in her memory. She thought of him constantly, of course, but only in terms of a vague, messy, generalized dread. She imagined him far away in a dangerous land, and forced the reality of distance to blur her memory. She'd worked herself to exhaustion to help her forget. Not once in the past two weeks had she cried. She wished that she could; perhaps the tight constricted feeling in her throat would ease, and she'd be able to breathe freely again.

Her gaze rose slowly from the delicate petals to the sight around her. The landscape was all monochrome, silver rain falling on an iron-gray sea. The city was oyster-white behind a veil of mist. She remembered the evening she'd stopped here to gaze at the sunset, on her way to meet Stu for the first time. She'd been dazzled by gold and green and vermillion, then; how appropriate now that her world was only shades of gray.

The lump in her throat grew larger but the tears refused to come. Her wretchedness was dry and scorched, and she was denied the soothing wash of tears. Her skin felt tight, stretched across her cheekbones; she was bloodless, desiccated, used up. She gripped the flowers harder, crushing the delicate petals, and the lilac smell intensified, filling the stale air of the car with sweet perfume.

Zan tossed the bouquet back onto the passenger seat and rolled forward. The rain drumming on her hood and streaking down her windshield mocked her with a release she couldn't obtain.

She gripped the steering wheel and stared ahead through the slanted rain with burning eyes. *If only I could cry...*

The rain seemed to be slackening by the time she got home, but it was impossible to park in her driveway, which had collected a slide of ankle-deep mud. Zan parked the Mustang along the road, hoping that a motorist wouldn't slide into it. The Sausalito hills were treacherous in a rainstorm.

Then again, she decided as she struggled down the muddy path with her briefcase and the flowers, that might be the only way to get rid of the car so that she could buy something a little more reliable. Maybe the house would slide down the hill as well, and she'd have to start all over again. She could forge a completely new identity.

As she fished for her keys she noticed a package leaning against the front door, thoughtfully covered in plastic by the postman. Bending down, she squinted at the return address. Iowa City. It was from her mother, then, and it felt like—Zan hefted it questioningly—a book.

She placed the package on the coffee table while she put the lilacs in a green glass pitcher and changed into dry clothes. Since her mother not only taught, but lived and breathed literature, she'd occasionally send her books by new writers she considered indispensable to Zan's continuing education. It was also, Zan knew, a sneaky attempt to bring her back into the fold. Her mother had been crushed when she had abandoned a fledgling but promising career in fiction to write her column for *Modern Times.*

Zan settled herself on the couch and ripped open the package, and a book tumbled out to fall on her lap. On the cover was a breathtaking photograph of steel-blue shadows on white snow beneath a navy blue sky. *Frozen with Wonder: Images of Alaska* was the title. Below that she read, *Photographs by Brody Flanders.*

Her heart seemed to stop as she stared at the letters that spelled out her brother's name. She turned the book over and over in her hands, unable to open it. Brody had mailed many of his negatives back home before he'd been killed, and her mother had told her that those last photographs were remarkable. But she'd never been able to bring herself to look at them. Over the years her mother had kept Zan up to date on her attempts to find a publisher for them, but her obvious discomfort with the topic had created some awkwardness between them. Gradually, her mother had ceased to talk about it.

Apparently she had finally succeeded. Zan reached inside the envelope for the letter she knew she'd find.

Dearest Zan,

I suppose you'll be surprised to see this. Perhaps the subject is no longer as painful for you. At any rate, I felt you should see the book.

The title comes from Brody's last letter to me. He wrote that he felt he'd done his best work in Alaska, despite the difficult conditions he'd encountered. You remember how he hated cold weather. "I may be frozen, Mom," he wrote, "but I'm frozen with wonder."

I don't know if you or I will ever truly get over Brody's death, but this book has helped me and I think it can do the same for you. I hope that you're ready to look at it.

Your latest columns have been wonderful. Have you written any fiction lately? Now don't bristle, I was only asking. I'll call soon.

Love, Mom

Zan's fingers trembled as she opened the cover to the book. She went through it slowly and with excrutiating care, barely moving a muscle except for her fingers turning the pages. Brody had been right; this was the best work he'd ever done. The photographs were extraordinary. He had always been a technically astounding photographer, but here his technique and his heart melded to produce stunningly powerful images. The land and the people who loved it had brought out something extra in him. They had brought forth an artist.

She had been so reluctant to look at these photographs for all those years; she'd imagined they would break a heart already strained from mourning. And they had broken her heart, but not in the way she'd expected. They'd broken her heart because they were beautiful.

Brody's death had been a horrifying tragedy but his life had held purpose. He had gone in a pure clean line to what he wanted to do and he had done it. He had died for it.

Brody was dead. But he had left behind a record of his strength and his joy, his astonishing capacity for pleasure. And now Zan realized why she hadn't been able to face these photographs. She had been angry. He had left her, and these images were the evidence of his desertion. They had killed him.

How could she have been so selfish, so horribly unfair? She'd taken everything personally; his life, his death. She'd found herself alone, without her protector, and she hadn't had the courage to let him go. Anger had kept him near her; so did sorrow.

Zan pressed her hands to her burning cheeks and discovered they were wet. Tears were sliding down her face, over her nose, into the corners of her mouth, dripping off her chin to land on her shirt. She was crying.

The hot tears stained the cover of the book she was clutching to her breast as she rocked back and forth, silent sobs wracking her body. She wept now for Brody as though she had never wept for him. For this time, she let him go. And finally, she wept for herself, for her cowardice and foolishness. It had led her to hang on to a distorted memory of the brother she had loved.

And it had led her to turn away the only man she'd ever wanted. Cowardice and pride had forced her to reject Stu before the desertion she'd imagined would come. She'd convinced herself he didn't take her seriously because to do the same for him would open her up to the possibility of a loss she couldn't face.

Zan sat staring at the book in her lap. Sometimes revelation came so quietly. "*I'm* the Bachelor of the 80's," she said out loud. "I'm the one who saves my commitment for my work, who tries to breeze through life as though it's a magazine article. I'm the jerk who's afraid to lay myself on the line."

Why couldn't she have asked Stu about his film deal, or given him the benefit of the doubt when he'd put off telling her about it? Because it had been a way to avoid him. It was the same reason she hadn't been able to face Brody's photographs. Anger and irony were a way to keep her distance, to keep her from feeling. And somewhere she'd known that she'd needed that distance, for somewhere she'd known that she loved him.

Zan stood up so suddenly the book slid off her lap and crashed to the floor. "I love him," she announced to the empty room. "I love him, I do." Relief and joy made her laugh out loud through her tears. She didn't care if he was in Arabia or Mozambique or Timbuktu. She'd keep on loving him, and she'd wait. The issue never was Stu's job, she would never deny him that. She knew that for herself to stop writing was to stop breathing. The issue in her mind had been the surrender to forces she couldn't control.

But love wasn't surrender, it was trust.

Zan began to pace. What could she do now? She had no idea where Stu was, or how to reach him, and she suddenly felt that if she didn't she would die. But if she did find out where he was, what kind of message could she send that could possibly convey how deeply she had changed, how irrevocably she loved him? Who could say that such an admission would be welcome to him? Had he ever really loved her at all? Who could love the cowardly jerk that she'd been?

As she paced in a panic from the fireplace to the front door, the bell rang. She flung the door open and Amelia, Bertie and Faye peered at her.

"Whatever is the matter, dear?" Bertie asked.

"I don't know, I—"

"You look very strange." Amelia patted her arm. "And we came over to give you such good news. They've found evidence of misconduct in Dwayne's handling of the funds, and he's agreed to give up control and fly off to Europe so they don't press charges."

"That's wonderful," Zan said.

Faye walked farther into the room and eyed the lilacs. "My, my, lilacs in November. That Stu is a marvel. Did he go all the way to the city to get them again?" She turned to the other women. "Remember that, girls? After the first town council meeting?"

"Poor Stu," Amelia said fondly. "So nervous about seeing you again."

"He was so worried about what you thought of him." Bertie smiled.

"What *I* thought of *him*?"

"Oh yes, dear. Said something about you thinking of him as a surly type with no sense of humor, or no sense of romance. So he took a poll at the Home."

"He asked us all what we thought was the most romantic flower in the world."

"Hush Amelia, I'm telling, now. So we all agreed on white lilacs."

Faye sniffed. "Actually, my suggestion was to forget the flowers and try emeralds instead."

"He had to go to five different florists before he found them," Amelia recalled. "Finally went to some fancy French place in the city."

Tears sprang to Zan's eyes. *"I just happened to see these on the way up here,"* Stu had told her. And she had poked fun at the lilacs in her column! How that must have hurt him. She'd only done it because the flowers had touched her, and she'd been afraid they'd just been a careless gesture.

"Oh dear, I think we've upset Zan," Bertie said.

"Are you all right, darling?" Faye asked gently, and Amelia patted her arm again.

"It's just that I love him so," Zan said. "And I can't tell him!"

"Why not, dear??"

"Because he's gone."

Bertie frowned. "No he's not. He's still here. Isn't he, Faye?"

"Yes, I talked to him a little while ago. But he's leaving tonight, isn't he, Amelia?"

"Yes. He's probably at the houseboat, packing."

Zan was busy lacing up her sneakers. "I'll try there first. Then I'll go to the airport if I have to." She grabbed her car keys and started toward the front door. "Do you know which airline he's flying on?" She bounced impatiently from one foot to the other as the women considered the question.

"Never mind. Maybe I can catch him at customs." Zan ran back to the coffee table, plucked the lilacs from the water, and ran back out the door. She took off down the path, barely hearing the women behind her.

"Customs? But Zan—"

"Zan, hurry up now!"

"Good luck!"

The rain slowed to a fine mist as she hurried to the car. Her heart pounding with her urgency, she slid behind the wheel and turned the key. The engine cranked obediently, then sputtered and died.

"Don't do this to me," she muttered through clenched teeth. She turned the key again savagely, and let out a moan of frustration as the motor refused to catch.

One more try brought no different results. Zan rocked back and forth in the seat and let out a muffled scream of frustration. Then she pounded on the steering wheel. Neither action provoked the engine into obedience.

Slamming the heel of her hand on the door handle, she shouldered her way out of the car and regarded it furiously. It was a symbol of her cowardice, of every mistake she'd made. She'd kept it out of some crazy, misplaced loyalty to a brother who would have been the first to laugh at her meaningless allegiance to a hunk of unreliable machinery. It was nobody's fault but her own that it was now about to completely ruin her life. She kicked it.

A low whistle stopped her from delivering another blow and spraining her foot. "That is some cool car."

Zan turned to find a blond on a ten-speed bicycle. He was gazing at the car with all the glassy-eyed adoration of a California male.

"Convertible too, man. Totally cool."

She looked at the car and back to the boy. "You want to buy it?"

"How much?"

She looked at the car again. "How much have you got?" she asked grimly.

The boy dug into the pocket of his jeans. Grinning, he held out ten dollars.

Zan took a deep breath. "Throw in the bicycle and it's yours," she said.

Chapter Twelve

Zan hadn't ridden a bicycle since she'd been in college. She wobbled down the steep hills, riding the brakes and skidding around corners. The lilacs she clutched against the handlebars streamed out a trail of white petals behind her.

Adrenaline was pumping furiously from sheer terror. She was terrified that she would miss Stu, and she was terrified that she'd break her neck on the way there. As she began to feel more confident on the bicycle she began to pick up even more speed. The thought of Stu's blue eyes compelled her, and by the time she turned the corner to pedal down the last hill she was practically flying.

When she hit a bump at the bottom she did go airborne for a moment; shrieking, she landed back onto concrete on her back wheel, bumped down on her front wheel, and sped on, tires squealing to avoid a parked car. She got a chorus of cheers from a group of teenagers at her daredevil antics, and she allowed herself a fast wave of acknowledgement before speeding on.

She reached the relatively flat street of Bridgeway with relief. Now it would just be some hard, fast pedaling to get to the houseboat. Her thigh muscles were beginning to ache with the effort but she kept up a steady pace. Traffic was snarled along the road beside her, and Zan reflected that she just might be making better time on two wheels. Perhaps that car had finally done her a favor after all. Or perhaps Brody himself had reached back to her to give her some badly needed pushes in the right direction.

Smiling at the thought, she wheeled around the last curve and bumped into Stu's muddy parking lot. She jammed on the brakes and the back wheel skidded, forcing her to jump off the bike to be able to stay on her feet.

She leaped straight into a mud puddle but she kept on moving, racing toward the docks. Her pounding footsteps on the wooden boards echoed the frantic beating of her heart. When she finally saw Stu's houseboat ahead, she nearly sobbed with joy and relief. Leaping onto the deck of the boat, her mud-encrusted sneaker slipped on the smooth surface and she skidded straight into the door. The force of her body propelled it open and she found herself spilled onto Stu's carpet, clutching a muddy bouquet of mangled flowers.

Stu looked up mildly from packing a suitcase, as if a frantic filthy woman crashed into his home every day of the week. When she said nothing, he scowled and looked grim. It was amazing, Zan thought, how alternately soft and hard his mouth could look. Right now it was pressed into a thin line. He looked mean and ornery, and she loved him.

She stood up uncertainly. "I sold my car."

"You did?" Stu asked, steadfastly polite and seemingly unmoved by the fact that she'd burst in on him after a devastating rift and imparted such irrelevant information. "I'm surprised," he went on, taking out a pair of socks from his suitcase. "I know how much it means to you."

"It doesn't mean anything anymore. Brody would have been the first person to laugh at me and tell me to sell the heap."

Stu nodded, his eyes puzzled, and continued to pack. He put the same pair of socks back in his suitcase, and that gave her courage. He couldn't be as cool and disinterested as he seemed. Or he could just be finicky about his socks.

She took a tentative step farther into the room. "Stu, I didn't come here to tell you about my car."

"Well I hope you didn't come to give me those flowers."

She looked down at the mangled lilacs. "I came to tell you that I'm an idiot."

"I see. After that statement, I think it might be better if I remain noncommittal."

"Oh, Stu." Zan sighed despairingly. "I don't want to banter with you anymore. I just want to talk to you." He looked at her warily, holding his socks, and she went on bravely. "I realized a lot of things today. Most of all, I realized that I've got to let go of what happened to me in the past. It's holding me back from the future." Zan took another step. There was no sign of encouragement on Stu's face, and fear snaked through her, making her weak. But she was done with cowardice, done forever.

"I never told you about my father," she went on softly. "It's because there's so little I know. He walked out on us when I was four years old. He never contacted us again. I guess that's why Brody and I became so close, and depended on each other so much. I know that's why I was so devastated when he was killed. And I know that's why I've developed this horrible fear of being left."

Stu looked down at his open suitcase, and back up at her, and she nodded. "Yes, I knew you would leave me. That's why I wrote that article, because I wanted to prove to myself that I didn't care. But I do care, Stu. If it's not too late, I want you to know that I'll wait for you to get back from the Middle East." She saw Stu start, but she went on, determined to say everything she'd come to say. "I've been unjust in so many ways. I should have realized that you would tell me eventually about your film. I shouldn't have kept this wall of irony between us. I've made the worst mistake anyone could ever make in this world. I've withheld my trust from the person who's most worthy of it, the person I love more than anything in the world. I love you, Stu."

She didn't know who moved first, or how they came together, but suddenly she was in his arms. They kissed as though it were the first time. They had nothing more to hold back, and the tenderness and passion could bank and build and they didn't have to quench it. It was a kiss of possession and belonging; it was a kiss of fierce, mad joy.

"God, Zan," Stu groaned against her mouth, her cheek. "I thought I'd never touch you again."

"Oh, you'll touch me again," she said, her voice brimming with happiness, "and again, and again, and—"

He silenced her with another kiss. "Now," he said when they drew apart, "I have some apologies to make too."

"You do?"

"Oh yes. That day I stormed in on you after I'd read your column. I think the reason I was so angry was that there were things in it that hit home. I thought I was being open and intimate with you, but I was withholding the most intimate fact of all: that I loved you. How could I blame you for turning away when I hadn't said those words?"

"But you knew then that you did?"

He smiled as her eyes searched his. "I knew almost from the beginning, but I didn't admit it to myself until after that first town council meeting. You showed me that night that I'd blinded myself to so much in life."

"Why didn't you tell me?"

"I tried, but I took the coward's way out. I relied on the thing that had kept me apart from the world all along: my film. When I cued that tape up for you I'd believed so firmly that you'd realize that I was telling you that I loved you. That was foolish. It was only because I was afraid to say those words myself. Then after that day I thought I'd been mistaken, that you didn't love me after all."

"As if I could help myself. I was just afraid of your leaving. Stu! What time is your plane?"

He looked at his watch over her shoulder. "Oh, it should be leaving right about now."

"But—"

"Don't worry, sweetheart. There's one every hour. Or I can leave tomorrow. Or you can come with me."

"Every hour? Me come with you?"

His lips grazed her eyebrow. "You see, you're not such an idiot after all. You got that all correctly."

Zan pushed him away. "Stu Temple, you tell me what's going on right now. A plane for the Middle East does not leave every hour. And you know very well I just can't pack up and—"

"Sweetheart, I don't know how you got this Middle East thing in your head, but I'm flying down to Los Angeles."

"Los Angeles? Aren't you making a documentary on a counterterrorism squad in the Middle East?"

Stu shook his head.

"Aren't you going halfway around the world for a year, possibly longer?"

He shook his head again. "I cancelled that project weeks ago, right after the first town council meeting, in fact. That's when I realized you were right, I should follow my instincts and go into feature films."

"But Jack said—"

"I didn't tell Jack until the deal was set. I was afraid he'd be disappointed, but he turned out to be thrilled."

"But Mark said—"

Stu grinned. "I told Mark about the tentative project in the beginning, just to make it clear that he couldn't extend the project. I forgot about that."

"But the man from Hollywood on your answering machine said—"

"You heard that message? So that's why you were so distant when I came back. The feature film is on the same subject. That's why it was so appealing to me. I could just deal with it in a dramatic format."

"You let me think for *weeks* that you were going off on this dangerous assignment..."

"Zan! I didn't know you thought that. I was waiting for the final meeting in Hollywood to talk with you about it. You know how tentative film deals can be. I had plans for us, but I wanted to be sure." He held her to him, and she felt him chuckle. "But I am touched to hear how you'd wait for me."

"I didn't say how *long* I'd wait," she grumbled into his chest. When she pulled away she noticed a streak of mud on his sweater. "Is my face dirty?"

Stu nodded soberly. "Your face is filthy, darling."

She flew past him to the bathroom and wailed when she saw her face in the mirror. It was streaked with mud. Stu lounged against the door while she turned the taps on full. "I can't believe you let me bare my soul to you while I looked like I just got back from a mud-wrestling competition."

He came up to hold her hair for her as she washed her face vigorously. "You've never looked more beautiful."

"Thanks. I think." When she turned, eyes shut and hands outstretched, Stu was there with a soft towel. "Now," she said from the depths of the towel, "is this going to be a weekend romance, or what? Are you shooting the film in Hollywood?"

"Part of it. And part of it on location in San Francisco and Rome."

"I guess I'll be waiting for you anyway."

"Not if I have anything to say about it. Don't you remember I said something about plans?"

She nodded. "As long as they include dinner tonight. I'm starved."

He slipped his arms around her. "Who's bantering now?"

"You're right. I'm a changed woman. No more smart-aleck remarks."

He hugged her fiercely. "Don't you dare change, Zan Flanders. I love every inch of you, every part of you, every smart-aleck thing you say."

"You must be in love," Zan said, but Stu interrupted her with a kiss. When they broke apart, she went on. "Seriously, Stu, there is one thing I've been thinking about changing. I think I should start writing fiction again. I gave it up after Brody's death. It was too hard to write about emotion in any real way. But I think I'm ready to now."

"And give up your column?"

"No, I'd miss it. You're right. I'm still a smart aleck at heart. Maybe take a leave of absence."

"That sounds perfect with what I have in mind."

"And what's that?"

Stu linked his fingers through hers and held up their entwined hands. "You and me. Like this, always. Whenever I look up, you'll be there. And I'll be there for you."

Tears filled her eyes. "Always."

"Which reminds me. Since you've helped me so much with my work, I want to help you, too. I've got the topic for your last column before you take a leave of absence."

She trailed her finger along his crooked nose and brushed back his jet-black hair. "And what might that be, love?"

"How about 'The Married Man of the 80s: Or How Stu Temple Rapidly Turned Into A One-Woman Man."